THEY TOLD US IT WAS HAUNTED

THEY TOLD US IT WAS HAUNTED

AMY-BROOKE ODELL

www.blkdogpublishing.com

To the friends, and the adventures.

Two got together when they both had another.
One took out their anger from the loss of a lover.
The last one tried to hang on to what was losing ground,
And when it couldn't be stopped?
He decided to tear it down.

Acknowledgements

They Told Us It Was Haunted could not have happened without
the support and encouragement from:

Brandon
My amazing boys; Dawson and Tuck
Mom & Dad
Chris & Lance
Nicky and the entire team at Blkdog
Loren, Tay, and Tracey
The relatable and witty Alison Grey
Ashley & Antwaun
Two amazing former teachers
And so many others.
Love.

PROLOGUE

It was just supposed to be a bit of fun on a balmy spring night. An adventure, a story to tell in years to come. But, if she were being honest, she would've kept that place tucked away in her mind, never to be thought of again. If not for the news that the house had sold.

1

Then

Four sets of shoes slap the wet asphalt as the group tumbles off the creaky wooden porch and catapult into the hazy night. Crackles from the officer's radio echo as he slides the flashlight beam over each of their faces. They don't make it past him or his cruiser. Defeated, they stop, hands on knees and chests, catching their breath.

"You kids want to tell me what you were doing in there?" The officer motions to the crumbling house set further back from the newer ranch-style home to the side of them. He raises an eyebrow, aggravated at having been called out here again. Every few months, here he is, catching thrill seeking kids messing around the creepy old place. He wishes the county would tear it down already.

"Just checking it out. Ghost huntin', ya know?" Derek answers. The officer is far less intimidating than the sirens announcing his arrival.

"Honestly, we're sorry. We weren't even in there for long. We didn't break in; the door was unlocked," a petite blonde named Whitney chimes in. She bats her eyelashes coyly at the tall and skinny policeman. She's terrified of getting arrested; what would her parents say? But she can't appear nervous; that will just make it worse. Her eyes trail to her group of friends as she discreetly attempts to straighten her shirt. "Anyway, we won't do it again." She looks to Ellie for confirmation. Something hardens in Ellie's eyes and it makes her uncomfortable. Whitney breaks the stare and looks down at the ground, studying the dirt caked on the sides of her sneakers.

A garbled message comes through on the officer's radio, and he steps away to respond, still eyeing the foursome. The four friends, Derek, Whitney, Ellie, and Jackson, nervously glance at each other, offering a few shrugs and shuffling their feet. It feels like ages before the officer returns.

He steps under the streetlamp, and they can now make out a name tag on his uniform: Warner.

"Yeah, sorry Officer Warner. We'll just go straight home if that's okay?" Ellie twists a long strand of black hair around her fingers. She prays her damsel act works, and the officer lets them go. She's desperate to keep him from going inside the home, and she's not the only one.

A light in a neighboring house comes on, catching everyone's attention. They turn to see a silhouette leaning forward toward the curtains. Either just a nosey neighbor, or the one who actually phoned the police. It doesn't matter. Let them watch. It's not like they are the only kids to ever try to go into the house. They've all heard the stories. It's not even their first time here at the house, but it is their first time getting caught.

Warner's eyes linger on the neighbor's window before turning to each of the kids across from him. They can't be more than nineteen, college freshman most likely. Townies from the looks of them. He guesses they all live around here and attend the university up the highway. He doesn't smell any alcohol, and their eyes appear normal. The one guy; the tall, tanned guy with the close shaved head, hasn't said a word. Warner wonders why.

"What's your name, kid?" He nods to the quiet one just left of the girls.

"Jackson."

Officer Warner nods and glances from face to face. "And the rest of you?"

Each one gives the officer their name, growing more worried by the second, until finally Warner's radio gives off another static-filled message, undecipherable to the group. He stares them down, intimidating them, before giving a shrug.

"Let this be a warning to you. Don't come messing around here anymore, abandoned or not. It's not only dangerous, but the neighbors will call again, and next time, I'll have to bring you in. Now, ya'll head on home."

The group lets out a collective sigh of relief, muttering their thanks as well as apologies. Each one of them is happy that the officer didn't decide to pursue the issue any further, each one with their own reasons. One person, in particular, is relieved that Officer Warner didn't see what they did inside of that house tonight.

2

Her long, yellow hair blows and tangles freely in the wind as Whitney Parker sails down the road, window open and one hand tapping the steering wheel in time to the music. The mid-November evening sunset casts everything in a warm, coral glow, and the scent of burning leaves and the last grass cutting of the year mingle together in a heady mix, floating through the open air. After the long, endlessly hot days of a North Carolina summer, there is nothing better than a brisk fall night to bring a sense of excitement.

"Have a good day, hon?" She glances in the rearview, taking in the sight of her beautiful, curly haired daughter Melody.

Melody is five years old and such a happy child. Completely unaffected by the fact that her daddy never comes around. Her daddy, who was all set to marry Whitney almost six years ago-that is until he found out that she was pregnant. A marriage he could handle, he claimed, a baby he could not. So, that's how it was. Just the two of them; mother and daughter. To be honest, Whitney has grown to prefer it that way. Sometimes in certain lights, Melody looks exactly like her daddy. Those times make Whitney's heart fill with sadness, but mostly, like right now, the sparkle in her yellow-blonde hair and the dimple shining on her right cheek are all Whitney, and Whitney can pretend that Mel is hers and hers alone.

Melody's eyes connect with her mother's in the rearview mirror, and she smiles and nods.

Attention back to the road, Whitney carelessly bumps over the hard steel of the train tracks, shaking her out of her thoughts.

"Sorry!" She cries as the car jerks them in their seats. She wraps her fingers around the steering wheel, promising herself to be more careful, pay more attention. Something brown floats up from the passenger seat, crowding her peripheral vision. Thinking it must be some piece of paper or trinket dislodged from her daughter's backpack, she haphazardly grabs at it, all the while trying to keep her eyes on the dusty road ahead. Content that nothing will jump out in front of her for the next two seconds, Whitney glances to the side.

Her screams ignite terror in her daughter's face; tears automatically fill Melody's eyes at the distress of her mom. The car bumps to the side and slides off the road in a skid of tires and a cloud of dust. Whitney flings herself out of the vehicle and over to her daughter's door in the back as fast as her legs will take her. Cursing loudly as she struggles with the door, she finally gets it open and rips Melody from her booster seat, knocking them both to the ground. She scrambles backward, daughter tightly held in her arms, shaking.

An older man; graying, and somewhere mid-sixties watches the commotion from his front porch. Not one to leave anybody in distress, he rushes across his yard over toward the road to see what he can do to help.

"You girls okay?" He calls out.

"S-snake!" Whitney cries, sliding back on her butt away from the car.

The old man looks to the ground, eyes sweeping the yard.

"In the car!" Whitney yells. "There's a snake in my car! Passenger side!" Melody remains quiet, both arms gripping her mother's neck.

Both mother and daughter watch as the kind man marches up to the passenger door, peering through the window. A loud smack at the car window causes him to jump back. "Look out. Copperhead!" He yells over his shoulder. The snake settles down into the seat before the man yanks the car door open and grabs ahold of the snake's tail in one lightning fast motion. Angry, the snake squirms and twirls, hissing and snapping its mouth. His fangs flash in the commotion. Holding the snake far from his face and chest, the older man races forward, slinging it far into the woods. Wiping his hands off on his jeans, he walks back over to the pair.

"What in the world were you doing with a copperhead in your car, miss?" He holds out a hand, helping them off the ground.

"I honestly have no idea how it got there." Whitney's face pales. She remembers rolling up the windows and locking the doors before going into work. It just doesn't make any sense, but maybe it somehow slithered in as she picked up Melody from school. It could happen, she figures. But, snakes don't just casually slink into a car daily. "Anyway, thank you so much for your help. You definitely saved us today." The color slowly returns to her cheeks.

"It was nothin'; you girls just be careful. A bite from that thing will send you straight to the hospital. Alright?" Their rescuer takes a few steps back toward his home, wiping his brow.

"We will. Thanks again." Whitney gives him a bright smile filled with a bravery she doesn't feel as she walks Melody back to the car to help her into her seat.

Once back at the driver's side, she finds her bravado gone. Exhausted and hesitant, she finally tells herself the snake is long gone, and she settles down in her seat. But the fear still grips her, and her eyes quickly scan the interior of the car, making sure the snake didn't leave any friends behind.

"Well, that was an adventure, I'd say. Why don't we go find us some dinner?" She winks to her brave little child patiently waiting in the back, the fear of the past few moments already put out of the little girl's mind. To be a child again, she thinks, and just let your mind skip right off to something else.

"Yes mam." Melody replies, gazing out of her window. She watches their unknown hero staring at them from his porch as they pull back onto the road.

Back onto the highway, Whitney listens to the latest tales of the kindergarten class as she turns to ease the car into a parking space in a local fast-food restaurant. Midland Chicken. Melody's favorite.

"Want to eat here or take it home?" Whitney asks although the answer is always the same. Midland Chicken has the kid's play area to put all others to shame, and Melody never misses a chance to go play.

"Here! Duh, mom!" Melody squeals, perking up tremendously.

Loaded down with a tray filled to the top with spicy fried chicken, french-fries, biscuits, and lemonades, the two pick their way to their favorite booth. Off to the side, slightly in the back, but still close to the play area. Quiet and out of the way. They stuff themselves full, leaning back in their seats, both satisfied from their meal. It takes no time for Melody to recover from her feast before she is off and running, throwing her shoes at an open cubby, and jumping wildly into the ball pit, squealing right along with the other children.

Her straw rattles against the remaining ice cubes as Whitney sips the last dregs of her lemonade, watching her daughter with a smile on her face. She can hear the excited shouts from where she's seated. That little girl is her world, and she loves to see her happy.

She lets Melody play for over an hour, chasing and giggling along with all the other kids. They are so free at this age, always excited to see a new kid running toward them. Happy to have as many friends as they can collect. Racing down slides, diving into the ball pit, and crawling through the netted jungle gym. But, it's been a long day and Whitney is growing tired. After much negotiation, she finally gets her sweaty and out of breath daughter out of the play area and back into her shoes.

It crosses her mind that Melody has a dentist appointment tomorrow afternoon that she had forgotten.

Debating whether to ask her mother to take Mel or to ask off work early, she isn't paying attention as she flings the door open to leave and bumps right into the very last person she ever expected to see on a Tuesday night at the local chicken place. Her foot catches on a crack in the flooring as she stumbles backward, clutching her daughter's arm.

3

"Oh my God. Ellie." Whitney's eyes widen as if she's seen a ghost. It's been nine long years since she last saw her old best friend. Not once did she imagine Ellie would ever come back home. As the shock wears off, she takes in the sight of her former friend – same striking eyes on the same blemish-free face. Still so beautiful. The long years away have not aged her one bit, Whitney begrudgingly realizes. Self consciously, she rubs at the wrinkles she's recently noticed on her own forehead.

Ellie's eyes dart around the restaurant as if searching for a quick escape. Finally, she turns her attention to Whitney. "Whitney! Wow, it's um, it's good to see you. And who is this?" A tan, slender hand points to Melody, bracelets jingling as she gestures. Ellie's voice shakes ever so slightly as she tries desperately to control it; she knew eventually she would run into some folks, but she didn't think it would be so soon. Not her first night back, and definitely not Whitney.

Two women who used to be best friends, who grew up together, no longer know how to act around each other. They used to be inseparable. For years, they spent every single day together; they took the same classes, their boyfriends were friends, and they basically lived at each other's houses. Even their parents were best friends. But, somehow, that night at the Doris house changed everything. It changed everyone. Sure, they all had another year together after that, but it was never quite the same. Too many secrets got in the way. What was once an unbreakable foursome filled with hugs and laughter and inside jokes had quickly turned into squinted eyes, sideways glances, and half-hearted shrugs. A quiet discomfort had settled over them, and they all spent that last year pulling further and further away from one another. Now, here they stand in the midst of the busy week-night dinner rush, awkward and uncomfortable.

"This is my daughter Melody."

Melody smiles proudly up at this woman that she has never met.

"Well, hi there, Melody. My name is Ellie. It's very nice to meet you." She leans down to speak directly to the adorable child in front of her. "I'm an old friend of your mother's." Her voice slightly cracks.

"Hi!" Melody squeals before whipping her curls over her shoulder and straining to look back to see what her friends are doing in the play area.

Ellie straightens up, staring just past Whitney's face and wanting nothing more than to just pick up her food and high tail it back to the motel alone, to be done with this awkwardness. She should have never come back. Something inside of her breaks just a little when speaking to the beautiful child who looks so much like the Whitney from their childhood. Things might have turned out differently for Ellie if she hadn't had to come back here.

"Well-" They both start.

Whitney chuckles. "I have to get Melody home and ready for bed, but it was so great to see you again! We really should get everyone together to catch up sometime. I'm sure the guys would love to see you..."

Ellie shrugs, noncommittally. "Yeah, I mean that sounds nice. I'm not sure how long I'll be in town though. Just passing through, you know? Anyway, we'll talk soon." She calls out as she is already sailing past Whitney and Melody and making her way to the food counter. She doesn't bother to ask about Jackson or Derek; she's long since convinced herself that she doesn't care. With her head up and her back ramrod straight, she forces herself to give off an air of someone who has it all together, not someone whose life is falling apart before her eyes.

The conversation with Ellie replays in Whitney's head on the drive home. Back then, she knew that Ellie wanted out of this town, but tonight, she got the feeling that it wasn't just the place her old friend wanted to get away from but her as well. But why would her former best friend want to leave all of her friends behind like that? Yes, they grew apart, but Whitney was still happy to see her, so why wasn't Ellie?

She checks the rearview mirror and notes her daughter sleepily playing a game on her tablet, so she decides to take the long way home and work through her thoughts. With one hand on the wheel and an elbow resting against the window, she turns down the curvy twists of the town's backroads. The sun sets early this time of year, and the deep purple of twilight blooms across the sky. Lost in thought over whether or not Derek and Jackson would want to see Ellie again, Whitney cruises up to the four way stop. Maybe she shouldn't have pulled away from everyone all those years ago. It got awkward; a strange shadow of secrets hovered around them. But, it wasn't just her that let go. She can't blame herself for something they all did.

The sun dips below the horizon, and the scenic country road is shrouded in darkness, but as she drives past the stop sign, her headlights bounce, reflecting off a yard sign. She does a double take and slows the car to a crawl. Looking in the rearview mirror, she notices Melody already sleeping. She pulls her car over to the side of the road. The large white and green **Farmwood Realty** sign rests right out front of Old Doris's house, and just above the sign hangs a bright red **SOLD** placard. Whitney's breath escapes her in a quick whoosh. It's impossible. No one has lived in this house since she was a child. Why in the world would someone want to buy it now? Honestly, it should probably just be condemned.

Although it rests between two other homes, the property boasts several acres behind the house. The dilapidated farmhouse looms ominously with a presence that belies its small stature. The curtain twitches from the house next door, sending Whitney into a tailspin of memories that she would rather not rehash. Images of a Saturday night with her four friends spent breaking into Doris's house, flood her mind. Her cell phone had vibrated over and over in her purse as she set the bag down and followed Jackson into an abandoned room. His smell was intoxicating, like campfire and gasoline, and she didn't care where Derek and Ellie had gotten to as he leaned her up against an old peeling wall.

A similar shadow emerged from behind a curtain as a nosy neighbor watched the police officer question them about being in the house. She just bets it was the same busybody that is watching her now. Whitney shakes her head, willing the images to scatter from her mind. A blush warms her cheeks; it's been a long time since she thought about that night with Jackson. They both were seeing other people, and they never let it happen again. They never told a soul, and she doesn't intend to now.

The curtain moves again, kicking Whitney into gear. She doesn't want to be seen around here. Not that anyone would remember her, but still, the place gives her the creeps—it always has. Her tires crunch the gravel as she pulls back onto the road. The soft snores from her daughter in her booster seat help to calm Whitney's frayed nerves. But she can't help feeling a darkness follow her the rest of the way home.

The car jerks into park and Whitney steps out on her driveway and into the emerging night. A shiver ripples down her back as she looks at her own rented townhouse. The house connected to hers is available and has been vacant for a while now. Usually, she likes the fact that it's empty. It's quiet, and she doesn't currently have to share the driveway or a wall with anyone else. But tonight, it's just lonely, and dark, so dark.

Melody softly mumbles as her mother unbuckles her from her seat and hefts her into her arms. She still can't hang on during a nighttime car ride, and Whitney swears she weighs ten pounds more when sleeping. Grabbing at her purse with one hand, Whitney smashes it under her arm as she struggles to close the car doors and lock them. The chill from the fall night cools the sweat that has formed on her brow, and in the distance, she hears the distinctive hoot of an owl. The feeling that followed her from that awful house just won't fade. She laughs wildly out loud at herself as she fumbles with the door lock; her place isn't scary. She looks out across the street to the other row of townhomes, a couple of them dark and a few dimly lit. Neighbors living their own lives, paying no attention to her. It's hard for her to tell if that makes her feel better or worse. It's just that seeing Doris's house again has her shaken up. She has lived in this home for almost six years. There's nothing to be afraid of. But then again, what a strange day with the snake in her car, running into Ellie, and seeing the house again. Her past is colliding with her present, and it's throwing her off-center.

Thankfully, Melody stirs awake as soon as the front door shuts. It'll be a nightmare trying to get her to bed, but she's been playing hard and needs her bath. Whitney sends the little girl to her bedroom to unload her backpack while she runs the bathwater, tossing in a little lavender scented bubble bath to help Melody rest. As she works the tangles from Melody's hair, she can't help thinking back over her encounter with Ellie. Melody closes her eyes and leans her head back as her mother pours warm water over her head. The suds swirl in the bubbly water.

"Can I play toys Momma?" The little girl asks, eyes bright even while tired.

"Sure, baby. Just a few minutes though." Whitney hands her the pail of bath toys before sinking down against the bathroom wall, watching as her daughter's imagination turns ordinary bath blocks into a mermaid cave and a rocket ship.

Suddenly, she can't be still. All of the events from the last few hours pour over her, making her skin itch. The urge to talk to someone grows intense. She pulls her phone from her pocket and scrolls through the names in her contacts until she lands on Jackson Gray. Her face flushes, and a soft buzzing grows in her ears. She can't. She scrolls back up, locating Derek's name. Undecided, she hovers her finger over it only momentarily. It's been almost a year since she last spoke to Derek. Even after losing touch with Ellie and Jackson, she occasionally saw him, but his old pushiness and playboy attitude had become too much for her to take. Still, he is her friend, and he should know about Ellie and about the Doris house. She stares at his name for a moment, a splash of bath water sprinkling her face and bringing her back down to reality. She takes another look at the screen before setting the phone down on the floor and reaching into the tub to pull the drain plug.

"Alright, little missy. Time to get ready for bed." Whitney helps her daughter out of the tub and wraps her into a towel. "Go to your room and put on some pajamas. I'll be there in a second." She stands, looking down at the phone as if it might jump up and attack her.

Thirty minutes, two stories, and a bedtime prayer later; Whitney closes her daughter's bedroom door behind her and retrieves her phone from the bathroom floor. As she sits down on her bed preparing what to say, the wind picks up outside. It rattles and hisses through her old drafty window. Something crashes outside and she jumps to her feet. *This is ridiculous. It was probably somebody's trash can, knocked over by the wind.* Without another thought, she presses the call icon and waits nervously as the phone rings.

"Whitney! What a surprise!" Derek yells into the phone. Whitney can hear the low roar of a crowd in the background. Derek, unmarried and unattached, is probably spending his evening looking for women at either a bar or club. "What in the world are you up to?" He sounds so completely at ease.

A brief hint of jealousy over Derek's lack of responsibilities washes over Whitney for just a moment. But then, her eye catches the framed portrait of her and Melody smiling in the sunshine in a field of sunflowers resting on top of her dresser, and she decides she loves her own life, exactly the way it is. Being a mother is what she loves, what she was made for.

"Hi, Derek. It's been a while, huh? Listen, I need to talk to you really quick. If you have a second…"

"Sure." The line crackles slightly. "Let me just step outside, kay?"

The phone crackles louder, sounding like it may have

been dropped and picked back up. A loud crunch on the line has Whitney wincing and contemplating hanging up. Forgetting the whole thing.

"Sorry, kinda loud in there. Anyway, what's up?" Derek has returned, and before she knows it, Whitney gets straight to the point. She unleashes a torrent of information over the line, starting with the snake and ending with that house.

4

Derek taps the red icon on his phone and wheels around on his heel, unsure of his next move. Five minutes ago, his life was fine, going along just as usual. And maybe it still is, but now it feels different, like there are eyes on him. He knows it's silly; nothing has fundamentally changed in the time he spoke to Whitney, but then... the information isn't even that strange; his old friend Ellie back in town, and an abandoned house finally sold. None of that is really all that weird. So why does he feel like it is? And that bizarre incident with Whitney's car? Just hearing her tell it gave him the creeps.

There's too much to sort through to go back inside, so, without so much as a goodbye to his buddies, he makes his way over to his own car. Suddenly, this place and these people—it's all too much for him. This is the last place that he wants to be, and he is relieved to have decided to use cash tonight instead of starting a tab on his card. No need to make excuses for his exit, he can just leave. He jumps in the driver's side. The gear shifter sticks for a second, but he manages to get it into reverse, only making it maybe two feet before slamming it back into park. It's dark inside the car. As shadows dance under the parking lot lamps, images of a copperhead lurking on Whitney's passenger seat send cold shivers down his neck and have him scrambling for the interior lights. Once satisfied that there are no snakes hiding out, he resumes his retreat from the noisy bar.

He makes his way through the misty streets of downtown Charlotte, wind blowing the trees back and forth and he contemplates what to do. He's shaken, and it took a lot of time and determination to build the crumbling foundation of his life on his own away from his former friends. One phone call and everything feels ready to collapse. It's been a couple of weeks since he's spoken to Jackson, but things are never awkward between them-it's like Jackson is the only one who didn't really change. Jackson was the one tether to their old group that he loosely held onto, an old steady. They keep in touch now and then but Derek keeps him at an arm's length away, he has to. Trying not to take his eyes off the road, he presses the home button on his phone. Between furtive glances at the road, he scrolls down the contact list until he finds Jackson's name.

Fifteen minutes later, Derek is flying down the old familiar back roads on his way to the Doris house, somehow drawn to it. He shouldn't go there, he knows that, but he has to see it for himself. With a sigh, he rests one hand on the steering wheel and the other on the gear shifter. The conversation with Jackson left him calmer, more level-headed. He is surprised that Jackson didn't know the house had sold. He lives so close; he must have seen the sign. But, maybe it happened recently. Maybe Whitney noticed the sign right after it went up. Who knows? In any case, he can't figure out why he and Whitney had such a strong reaction to the news- it didn't seem to faze Jackson. Nine years have passed since they all went inside that house. He has no idea who bought the place. It shouldn't matter. There should be nothing weird about it. But for some reason it does and there is. Perhaps it's just guilt--not a feeling that he is altogether familiar with.

The tires screech and skid on wet leaves as he slams the brakes, realizing that in the whirlwind of his thoughts, he almost drove right past the house.

But, there it is; the tired, white-washed, miniature farmhouse resting in all its horrifying glory. Derek didn't think it was possible, but the place looks even worse than it did so many years ago. Half of the graying wooden fence has buckled and rotted; slick ivy snakes its way through the sunken-in slats. The small front lawn displays a haphazard mowing job skirting around the trees. The shine from the streetlight doesn't stretch to the back acres, but it's not a stretch to guess that it hasn't been mowed in a very long time. Stuck in a time warp while the other nearby homes continue to be updated and loved. The years certainly have made their mark on the place, but it was always one paint chip away from being condemned. He's not even surprised that no one has fixed it up. It's hard to envision what it will look like once the new owners are finished with it. He wonders if they've heard the stories.

The car's headlights reflect off the white "sold" sign, blinding Derek briefly before he shuts them off. The glare fades and he reclines in his seat, taking in the strange house. His parents live close by—walking distance, but on principle, he always takes the longer way around to visit them now. Although he's only actually been on the property twice, the house had a way of weaving itself through his childhood and rerouting his life. Keeping this place far from his thoughts, he hasn't been back in so long. Not since that night nine years ago when his plans got so messed up. He still wonders sometimes if the police showing up and interrupting him was a good thing or not. Would the end result have been worth it? But something had to be done. All he wanted was to bring his friends back together. It was a temporary lapse in judgment, not who he actually is, he thinks to himself. He's rationalized it every day since.

His fingers drum a random beat on the steering wheel as he tries to clear his mind of those dark memories. He has a full life; no shortage of dates, lots of new friends—no one very close but he doesn't need that. His job is steady, it pays well, and he owns his own place. But even back then, as a student with no job, his life was good. His life has always been easy. He was a golden kid; everybody knew one growing up. One of the lucky few that just had it; they were never awkward, and things always went their way. Invisible flecks of gold floated down around them like they were chosen for it, that kind of grace that you can't force. It's what made the other kids love him, all the while being insanely jealous of him. There was no reason to try to hold on so tight, but he did it anyway.

His hands tremble, and he shakily removes them from the steering wheel, focusing on every inch of the house that everyone has always called; "haunted." Something moves in the corner of his eye; he follows the movement. A curtain at the neighbor's house billows in the partially open window. There are no lights on in that house, but he can still see white lace curtains masking a silhouette from the front room. The last time he saw that curtain move in the night was when the police came. He thought they would stick together. Instead, he found himself alone in a dark room; they all just kind of separated. He knew what he had to do, but then the sirens sounded and they all panicked. He remembers the way he could swear he heard a sound as the unlit match hit the floor. That feeling of relief when the officer was called away before having the opportunity to investigate.

No, he tells himself. No, he won't go back to that place in his mind again. It's over and nothing happened. The house is being sold, and someone else will rebuild and make wonderful memories here. Memories that have nothing to do with him, and he will put this place out of his mind for good. He will meet with the others just to see how Ellie is doing, and then, he will return to his own normal life. He won't go digging up the past.

Another jerk of the neighbor's curtains jolts him back to reality. The tires of his old 2000- something Mustang screech, sending dust swirling up into the night as he throws the car into drive and soars out of there.

As he drives, his mind conjures up the old spooky stories the children used to tell about the house. The kids he grew up with have been spreading them ever since they were in elementary school. No one ever went to that place unless it was on a dare, and even then, half the stories he's heard he can't be sure are true. With its already caved-in porch, chipped paint, and looming shadows in the dark, the place was ripe for urban legends whether or not they were real. The tales the grade school children spun were tame, usually about an old witch named Doris who lived in the house scaring off anyone who tried to enter. Derek himself used to walk by with his friends on chilly fall mornings, trading made-up stories, knowing that he had never even been brave enough to set foot in the front yard of the dismal house.

When he was in high school, it was like they were all playing a huge game of telephone. The stories had grown far more outlandish, more terrifying. Passed down from older siblings and retold countless times. By this time; Doris had passed away, kicking the fear factor of the place up a notch. A kid in Derek's gym class, Kris, claimed that he once went inside with his cousin. He said the place was your average abandoned house – dingy, unloved, unkempt, and littered with out-of-date furniture. Kris claims that they were just about to write the house off when the sounds began, an awful screaming coming in from every angle. Every time he got to that part of the story he clammed up, said he couldn't say anymore, that it was too much to talk about. The only thing he would say is that whatever happened there was so frightening that his cousin hasn't spoken a word since. Completely stopped speaking. Of course, none of the other kids believed him, especially since his cousin was visiting from out of town. He lived in some little place down in South Carolina, so no one could talk to him to verify the story. It all seemed pretty convenient to Derek and his friends. Kris's cousin never really came around after that, and a couple years later, Kris's dad was transferred to another duty station in the Army, so his family moved to Virginia.

Kris's story became another tale in the collection of anecdotes that no one believed but continued to pass on anyway. After all, the old house was so imposing. They felt it their duty to keep the spirit of the ghost stories alive even if no one really thought them true. What other scale could the teenage boys hanging out in their friends' basements use to prove their bravery? Never one to be outdone, Derek once gathered around a group of freshmen boys, testing himself to see if he could come up with a story more frightening than Kris's. A sort of game for him. He leaned in close, whispering to the boys that he once visited the house. He told them that he walked right up to the front door and knocked loudly, but before anyone could answer the door, it swung open all by itself. He delighted in the attention as he lied about walking in and seeing a wild-eyed Doris in a ripped nightgown, white hair flowing down her back, standing faceless in the center of the living room. All around her, the walls were dripping with fresh blood. The terror in their eyes gave him such a power rush. He did that, he created that reaction.

Eventually, after his class refused to stop nagging their home-room teacher about it, Derek learned that Doris, a woman in her late 80's who had been a widow--died of complications due to old age in that house, which had been owned by her family for years. Shortly after, the place was sold to a couple with three children. They weren't there even a year before the father suddenly took a new job out of state. At least that's what Mrs. Fulton said. He later heard that the house was sold back into the original family although no one ever moved in. It all sounded so normal. Who was Derek to question it; let the house just be fodder for teenage entertainment. It was still fun to make up the stories, to walk by it on Halloween, a cute girl by his side.

Releasing himself from his memories, Derek sails down his driveway desperate to be home. He is enveloped in a deep quiet as the car shuts off, but instead of rushing inside, he leans his seat back and stares up through the sunroof at the clouds that wash over the moon. His mind races, bringing up dozens of conflicting thoughts, and he wonders what Ellie looks like today. After all, it's been a long time. She was always the hardest to read--not open like Whitney or easy-going like Jackson. Just wound up and closed off. Only randomly letting cracks into her real personality shine through. He thinks of the stark contrast of her long, flowing, black hair, and seafoam eyes and wonders if she has aged at all. Has that sparkle in her eyes dulled over time? Has she found anyone that she can be herself around? If she was so desperate to leave, why come back?

5

The harsh blue cast of the light fixture in her small hotel room is so jarring after driving in the dark, that Ellie has to step back for a moment and get her bearings. You would think the local motel would use the warm-toned LEDs instead of these severe hospital style ones. It makes the whole ordeal of coming back that much more depressing, a spotlight on her biggest failure. Losing her job was bad enough, but to have to come home, tail between her legs, is the worst thing she could imagine, and now she's living it.

It was amazing for a while. She loved everything about living in Minneapolis, everything except for the weather. Growing up in North Carolina doesn't exactly prepare you for a Minnesota winter. But, she loved her little apartment in the city, and she loved her job. Being a junior furniture designer for a large company was a dream. It was a job she had truly worked hard for, and Ellie was a shining star--she was on her way to quickly promoting to designer. It changed her perspective; she was no longer running from her past. Instead, she was running toward her future. For the first time she was beginning to believe in herself. But then, it all came crashing down in spectacular fashion, and instead of promoting, she wound up fired.

Losing her job meant losing her beloved apartment, and to make matters worse, it's either staying in this motel or with her parents. It may have been nearly a decade since she left home, but they could have at least kept her bedroom for her. Her eyes roll at the thought of all of the showy, overpriced workout equipment filling up the space. They could have used the guest room for that, but for some reason they chose to leave that room alone. With a pout she slams the door behind her, fully aware that just being in town is bringing back all of her old irrational teenage angst. She might not even tell them that she's back. Anyway, she's only here for a little while, no reason to barge in and get them all worked up, except for the fact that she really does love her parents and has missed them every day since she left. Besides, she may need money soon, once her severance runs dry. Hopefully, it won't come to that. There is nothing she hates more than asking for help.

Her room in the motel is cramped, but at least it's on the third floor. The place has a small lobby with a breakfast bar and an elevator. It's a good thing because not only is it in her budget, but Ellie has a fear of motel rooms with door access right off the parking lot.

She tosses her bag of take-out chicken onto the small wooden desk and shrugs out of her jacket and shoes, leaving them both in a heap by the foot of the bed. The first thing she did after checking in this afternoon was hit the vending machine, so she glances at her soda options in the mini fridge and takes one out.

The swivel chair groans as she plops down into it and swirls it around to turn on the television. Once she settles on a channel playing reruns of one of her favorite sitcoms, she dives into her now lukewarm food. It's greasy and could stand to be reheated, but it tastes pretty good and feels like home. Plus, she hasn't eaten anything since grabbing a quick banana earlier.

Just as Ellie is polishing off her last couple of fries, her cell phone, resting on top of the motel's stationary beside her, lights up. *Derek.* She chokes on a fry. That's a name that hasn't graced the screen of her phone in quite some time. She hits the red ignore button without hesitation and takes a long swig of her soda. *Whitney sure has a big mouth.* Apparently, she didn't make it clear enough that she doesn't want to resurrect past friendships. She just wants to plan her next move, apply to a few jobs as far away as possible, and get the hell back out of here.

Outside, the wind whistles loudly, drowning out the canned laughter from the t.v. and shaking the windowpane. It sounds like a storm is kicking up, the kind of storm that usually hits this part of North Carolina late in the summer, not typically in the fall. Ellie loves the storms, something about the noise and commotion helps her sleep, making her feel safe and cozy inside and tucked away from the elements. With a glance to the bed and back at her now unappealing chicken, she decides she's had enough. She balls up her wrappers and napkins and tosses them into the trash, ready for a warm shower and a soft bed. The small hotel bed seems inviting with its standard white sheets and thick comforter. It may just be the weather but either way, she can't wait to collapse in the bed and let her thoughts go.

The stream of hot water from the shower hits her back and runs down her long hair. Her shoulders fall, relaxed for the moment. A strong clap of thunder rattles the room, making Ellie drop the bottle of face wash in her hand. Her eyes burn as she tries to rinse off her face quickly. As much as she enjoys a good storm, she doesn't care to be caught in the shower while it's lightning. After a brief struggle with shutting off the water, she is out and warm in her terry cloth sweatpants and Sherpa sweater. With a look of disdain at the built-in hair dryer, she leaves the bathroom, towel drying her hair. It's too long and she is too tired to be bothered with drying it tonight. Never the one prone to tidiness, she discards the towel on the floor, tossing it carelessly, much the same as her shoes and jacket from earlier in the evening.

After the hot shower, the bed looks warm and inviting, and Ellie can't wait to drift off and forget about her wretched day, to just go to sleep instead of replaying all the ways her life plan has gone awry. She hits the light switch, plunging the room into darkness. The abandoned cell phone glows from its spot on the desk. She grabs it and scans her messages.

As she makes her way to the bed, something small

and fuzzy skitters across her foot. Immediately, the hair on the back of her neck stands on end. Not a fan of creepy crawlies of any sort, Ellie flicks her foot, flinging the creature off. Racing to the light switch, she flips the lights back on and scans the worn carpet. There, on the floor by the nightstand is a long-legged, brown spider; with fat black splotches splattered across his back. It's at the very least, the size of a half dollar coin. Heat warms her neck, and she stifles a scream. Backing up carefully, she looks around for something she can use as a weapon. There's nothing close by, and she's terrified to take her eyes off of it for fear that it will get lost in the room. Risking a quick glance, her sight lands on the stack of disposable coffee cups resting on top of the dresser. She snatches one up and creeps closer to the spider. How she wishes she had someone else to do this for her. Her hand shakes with revulsion, the cup unsteady, as she inches closer and moves further down toward the floor. Positioned directly in front of it, she lets out a deep breath, closes her eyes, and lunges, slamming the cup down on top of one of her biggest fears. The cup sticks a little in the carpet as she tries to slide and lift it without trembling. Once satisfied that the spider is indeed inside the cup, she thrusts it out as far away from her body as possible and races to the bathroom, flushing the horrifying thing down the toilet. With a sick kind of enjoyment, she watches the creature swirl down the bowl and off into the abyss.

It's just another checkmark on the list of bad luck lately, and now, Ellie is exhausted from the adrenaline and fully ready to go to bed, forgetting everything about this whole day. At this point, staying up any longer is probably just tempting fate. The comforter is soft as she slides under it in the calm of the dark and rests her head on the motel's surprisingly fluffy mountain of pillows. The combination of clean skin and fresh sheets feel delicious on her skin.

Her leg itches. She scratches it with her other foot and snuggles down deeper. But, her leg itches again and once more on her thigh. Something crawls across her right ankle; she jerks her leg up just as pure fire shoots through her back. She's been bitten or stung, she isn't sure, but she flies out of the bed and across the room, swatting at herself every step of the way. Fear spreads through her, and goosebumps explode down her arms. She puts as much distance between herself and the bed as she can. Twirling around like a madwoman; she feels tiny little legs crawling over every inch of her skin. The desk lamp is close by so she hobbles over to it and grasps the switch, illuminating the room in the soft glow.

She's afraid to look but knows that she has to. That was more than just a bedbug bite. Velvety brown spiders scatter terrifyingly across the sheets. The bed is teeming with what must be a hundred or more of them, crawling over each other and shuffling under the pillowcase. The scream that builds from the pit of her stomach could shake the walls. There are too many spiders to see what kind they are, and Ellie doesn't plan on sticking around to find out. One falls from her hair, and she lets out another ear-splitting wail, swatting at herself until she is sure there are no more spiders on her body.

Barely taking the time to throw her strewn clothes back into her suitcase, she tears out of the door to demand a different room. Frightened guests peek from around their doors to see what's caused all the screaming as she runs wildly down the hallway with hot tears sliding down her cheeks.

6

Four red zeros blink back and forth, over and over, on the microwave. It's been that way for weeks now, and Jackson has yet to bother himself with resetting it. The power went out with the last big summer storm; some crazy wind and rain, remnants of a hurricane that blew through farther down south. The power was restored but resetting all of the clocks was something Jackson just hasn't found the energy to do yet.

Sitting in the dark with only the glow of his laptop and a small lamp in the living room behind him, Jackson works at the dining table. Rain drives down onto his roof as he stares at an excel spreadsheet pouring over figures, expenses, and profits from his landscaping business. A sigh escapes his lips as he lets his head fall into his hands. The worried, pinched tone in Derek's voice when they spoke earlier; it brings up a lot for Jackson. Sure, he was calm, even dismissive about the whole ordeal. But when he heard about Whitney... A snake in her car? While they may have never actually dated and only hooked up that one time- that night in the house, he feels a strange protectiveness about her. He always has. It's been a long time since he has even seen Whit, but hearing that something like that happened to her, it makes him want to rush over and take care of her. It's been nine years; why that feeling has come on so strong, he has no clue.

Derek was freaking out, making all kinds of wild

connections and assumptions. Theorizing about why Ellie is back, about the snake, and did Jackson hear about the Doris house selling? Of course, Jackson knew the house had been for sale. After all, he had made an offer on it. Not that he would mention any of that though. Jackson was finally able to calm him down, but only after agreeing to try to get the group back together soon. He can't help but think that Derek was only truly Derek when he was with their friends, leading the pack. But now that they have all gone their own ways, Derek is just out there floating, lost, not really knowing who he is anymore.

Of course, that's not a fair assumption- that house affected all of them. Anyone else would think that nothing really happened that night, but somehow, being in that house changed them. It gets into your mind. It wasn't like some demon came out of the coat closet and grabbed them, nothing that in your face. In fact, Jackson might be the only one who actually saw something that night, but he won't let himself dwell on that image. He can't be sure of it anyway. It's more that he could tell that everyone ran away from that place carrying more secrets than they went in with. His and Whitney's is a shared secret, but Ellie and Derek's remain a mystery. It's what drove them all apart. Being with Whitney complicated things especially since neither of them were single at the time. It might have been the romantic idea of being in a spooky haunted house forbidden to them that brought them close, or maybe it was always bound to happen. But, having secrets hovering between them all like an electrical charge was a strange feeling that they couldn't get past. It was the very first time since they all became friends that there was something between them that they weren't willing to talk about. And none of them knew how to handle it.

He slams the laptop closed, no longer able to concentrate. Whispers of long tucked-away images linger in his mind. He isn't sure what he saw that night, and it's been such a long time. Memories can be tricky. Besides, if what he saw was actually there, then he would have heard about it on the news. No, he tells himself. No, he didn't see anything that night, he was just playing into the fear of the "haunted house." That's all it was.

There was just so much going on that night. It was loud; there was shouting, banging, and screaming. He assumed the screams came from Ellie and that she was either pulling a prank or just scared and trying to find them. The air crackled with mystery and a welcome fear, the excitement of walking arm in arm with someone through a haunted trail on Halloween. Nervous giggles after a frightened jump. For him, the noises faded into the background; his teenage self couldn't be concerned with any of that with Whitney standing right in front of him. Then, the sirens came, the banging stopped, and everyone somehow just found each other and raced back out of the front door. It was on his way out that he ran past the old, worn-down dining room. The room was covered in dust, white sheets, and scattered chairs, and as he ran by, Jackson turned to look inside. It was really more of a quick glance; he can't be positive it was even there, but that exhilaration he felt was gone.

He stands up, forcefully sliding his chair back under the table, and paces the kitchen. It was just the creepy atmosphere in the house, that's all. He didn't actually see anyone's leg sticking out from under the table that night. He didn't. It was just his imagination. It had to have been because if it wasn't, then why didn't he tell the police?

7

A tangled web of sheets twist around Ellie's legs. She kicks them off and scoots up against the headboard, shielding her eyes. The curtains do little to block out the bright morning sun. It's a wonder she was even able to go to sleep after the spider horror show she endured the night before; honestly, the motel will be lucky if she doesn't sue. Had there been any other place with as good of a price, she would've been out the door. She runs her hand over the lump of pillows beside her until she makes contact with her phone. One new message. She could have guessed; it's a text from Whitney.

What a great surprise running into you last night! We should get together soon.

Sinking back into her pillows, Ellie thinks about it for a moment. She has no interest in playing catch up with her old friends. It's been too long, and they pulled away when she needed them the most. She won't feed into the fakeness of it all, sending cutesy little emojis over text. Besides, she never wanted to come back here. How embarrassing to have to tell everyone that she lost her job, or how she lost it. But, on the other hand, since things didn't pan out so well in Minneapolis, it might be nice to have some familiar faces to talk to. She chews on her bottom lip, an old habit that comes out when she can't seem to make up her mind.

She could lie. That's it, no one has to know why she came back home. Nobody knows anything about her life to say otherwise, and anyway, it's none of their business. She could say that it's because she missed her family, maybe someone is sick and they needed her. No, that could easily be disproven. It hits her; why not just go with something simple? The simplest lie is usually the most believable. She hasn't been home in so long, and she decided to come back on her vacation time. She'll tell them she's racked up two weeks of vacation, and she just wants to spend it here. She'll have a new job and place to live within two weeks. She will make sure of it.

Now that her story is settled, she wonders if she even wants to see them. They were her closest friends for so long; of course, she misses them. But she was at her worst when they went to that house, and they knew. The transition to college hadn't been as easy for her as it had for them, they all witnessed her struggles. She thought they were going to cheer her up, get her mind off of things, but it wasn't like that. Everyone really was so selfish back then, and they probably still are, she thinks. Derek never wanted to talk about the heavy stuff. He only wanted to be their connecting force, the center of their orbit. He was the leader and he decided what was important.

As for Whitney, Ellie saw the way that Whitney looked at Jackson when she thought no one was watching. They stepped foot in that door and Whitney took off after Jackson. The two of them pretended to go different ways inside the house, only to end up together in the back bedroom. For once, Derek wasn't able to keep track of everyone's whereabouts. Strangely, he ran off by himself; otherwise, he would've seen what Ellie had done. Ellie's cheeks redden with past hurts. Whitney never even told her about going off with Jackson. They were supposed to be best friends, as close as friends could possibly be. They had always told each other everything: every embarrassing moment, every secret, every everything until then. What a betrayal it was to have a boy who was like a brother and her best friend go off together like that and never even mention it. To make it worse, after that night, it was like Whitney had suddenly outgrown her. She broke up with her boyfriend and didn't even talk to Ellie about it. She was never available to hang out anymore, never wanted to talk, never answered calls or texts. She just pulled away, leaving Ellie wondering why. And now she wants to cheerfully introduce her daughter and send these bubbly text messages like nothing ever happened? Maybe this time, Ellie should be the one to push them away.

Her lips twist into a smile as she types her reply before tossing her phone to the side.

Super busy, we'll see!

It might have taken a while, years in fact, but now she is the one with the upper hand. Anyway, she is too busy. There are plans to be made; she has to start looking for a new job and town to live in and fast. Driven by the desire to run again, she hops up and grabs her laptop from her bag, taking it back to the bed. No one said she couldn't be comfortable while on the search.

An hour later with two motel coffees sending her brain buzzing; she has perfected her resume. It really showcases her strengths and it's mostly all true. A lot of her old co-workers were really into the LinkedIn app for networking and job searching, she downloaded it once but never kept up with it and ended up deleting it, but it may come in handy now on her hunt for a new career. She finds her phone now tangled in the mess of sheets and opens the app store, quickly downloading it and humming to herself. Hopefully, this makes things easier this time around. But she probably shouldn't use her last position as a reference. After all, she found a decent job once, she can do it again.

Her notification bar lights up across the top of her phone screen, interrupting the flow of setting up her profile. One new text message. From Derek. She rolls her eyes and pulls up the message.

Hey guys, I'm working out of the office today. Anyone want to meet up at Lake Shore?

Oh great, she thinks. She's been back home for exactly one day and suddenly found herself back in a group text with these guys. It's what she wanted so many years ago, to still be included, but she knows it's all surface stuff-they don't really care. And what, she is supposed to just go back to their old hangout like the past nine years never happened? Lake Shore Coffee Shop was their place. If they weren't gathering at one of their dorms or houses, they could always be found clustered tightly around an outside table no matter the weather, heads together, laughing like mad.

Her phone dings again.

I'm at work but it's a half-day. Mel has a dentist appointment at 1, I'm free after.

So, Whitney is in. Ellie doesn't know how to respond. She wants to say no, but she also wants to wait and see how Jackson responds. There's really no reason to meet up, nothing to talk about, and it took her so long to get past everything. They all stuck around here; she'd probably just feel out of the loop all over again. It's best she just doesn't go. That settles it. No waiting around. She pulls up her keyboard and types out a quick response.

Sorry! Can't make it. Loads of work stuff to wrap up today.

There. For once, she isn't chasing after them. Let Derek try to control everyone now.

8

Jackson eases his truck into a parking spot just across from the coffee shop and cuts the engine. The clock on the dash reads 2:50 P.M. He doesn't even want to be here and yet somehow here he is ten minutes early. It's not that he's avoiding his old friends, it's just the awkwardness of it all. After the way they all broke apart, it's hard to tell what's okay to talk about and what's not. They only know each other by who they used to be, not who they are now. He keeps in touch with Derek enough, but the chance to see Whitney was too tempting to turn down. He tells himself that he just wants to make sure that she is alright, that it has nothing to do with that one dimple that creases her left cheek when she smiles.

A petite blonde in a knee length eyelet dress walks past his truck, digging for something in her purse. Jackson sucks in a breath; he would recognize Whitney anywhere. She's still just as adorable as ever. Her soft, blonde curls bounce at her shoulders as she walks by, oblivious. He watches as she goes inside, not wanting to break the moment just yet. In his mind, he still sees her, radiant in her cap and gown, the day they graduated college. She had breezed past him, calling out "congrats!" They should've all been celebrating together, but as she passed, her smile never reached her eyes, and her dimple never showed. Sighing deeply, he jumps out of the truck, slams the door, and heads inside to meet the group.

The line is short, and he quickly spots Derek and

Whitney seated at the outside tables through the window. Their old table. He grabs his usual order – large coffee, black, with two stevia packets – and makes his way to the back door.

It may be a cloudy fall afternoon, but as he walks over to the wrought iron table, Whitney's sage green eyes turn his way and sparkle like they are lit directly by the sun. Derek, on the other hand, looks a little stiff in his button up shirt and khakis. Standing quickly, Derek pats Jackson hard on the back.

"So glad you made it man; it's been a while."

The paper coffee cup is almost too hot to hold, and Jackson struggles to keep his coffee from sloshing over and burning his hand. "Yeah, it sure has." Though he is speaking to Derek, his eyes slide to Whitney, his gaze holding for far too long. "How've you been?"

Her face flushes, and Derek either doesn't notice the silent exchange or just chooses to ignore it.

"Doing great. Job's good, you know, super busy. We really need to get together more often. How have you guys been?" Derek fidgets with the lid on his cup.

Jackson smiles at his old friend; it doesn't seem like too much has changed in Derek's world since they last spoke. "That's great, good; there's always work to do. That's about it these days." He glances back at Whitney who has remained curiously quiet during the whole exchange and raises his eyebrows at her.

"Oh, well I'm doing alright. Melody is great, growing up so fast. She's at her grandmother's house now, but she's so smart and getting so tall…" She trails off, not really knowing what to say.

"That's really good to hear." Jackson tells her.

"Totally." Derek speaks up. "So, the Doris house, crazy right?" He scratches behind his ear. "Who would have thought that place would ever sell? I swear, I thought they would eventually tear it down. Condemn it or something."

"I don't think I could buy it, not after knowing she died there." Whitney shivers, her hair cascading around her.

"Yeah, but it wasn't for any like, sinister reason. Besides, I don't think they even have to disclose that sort of thing." Derek takes a long slug of his coffee, finishing it off and crushing the cup in his hand.

"They don't." Jackson's eyes grow wide, realizing he actually spoke the words out loud. He could be imagining it, but Derek and Whitney watch him a little too intensely. He fiddles with his phone, trying to take the focus off him.

"I know nothing really happened, but after we spent just thirty minutes in that place, I was so creeped out I definitely wouldn't want to live there. Maybe it's not haunted, but I felt so weird after we left." Derek admits.

"I kind of did too. Actually, I still don't like to think about going to that place." Whitney mashes her lips together and stares at her feet. She had been happy to spend time with Jackson in the house that night, but it had complicated everything, and she has never admitted to anyone the strange feeling the house gave her. Like it was watching her, judging her. There were no ghosts to be seen while they were there; she knew the noises and rattles came from her friends. So how could she explain the uneasiness that settled like a rock in her stomach and continues to live there, resurfacing every time she goes back to that night in her mind?

She steals a glance at Jackson, still tapping away on his phone. She can't see that he is re-reading the email from James at the realty office letting him know that his offer on the house had been rejected. A higher bid came in. He studies the words for a moment before putting his phone away and asking Whitney about her run in with the snake.

Eventually, after discussing all of the different ways that a snake could come to sneak inside of a car, the conversation switches to Ellie.

"I don't know." Whitney sighs. "She really didn't seem all that excited to see me. I'm not sure that she will want to meet up."

"She was probably just tired or busy. I'll talk to her; she'll come around." Derek's old controlling nature peeks through his relaxed façade.

Jackson shrugs, not understanding why it matters if she comes around or not. The thought instantly makes him feel terrible-she was one of his best friends. Actually, she *was* his best friend—as close as siblings. But none of them acted the same after leaving that house. In any case, Ellie took off as soon as she could without so much as a text goodbye. If he were being honest with himself, her brush off hurt deeply. He had always thought that the four of them were strong; their friendship could survive anything. The past nine years proved him wrong, and time had only made him bitter.

Derek checks his watch; a brown leather Movado with an all-black face. A little flashy but classically handsome, much like himself. "Well, I hate to, guys, but I have to run. I have a late meeting. We'll do this again."

"Oh God. It's already six. I've got to go get Melody." Whitney stands quickly. Her chair rocks, dangerously close to tipping over. The strap of her purse slides down her shoulder. She smiles at Jackson as she fixes it.

Jackson stands as well. "Alright, well, I'll see you guys."

Derek and Whitney exit through the small metal gate leading out of the shop's outdoor area and go off their separate ways to their own cars, leaving Jackson standing alone, eyes lingering on Whitney's retreating figure before once again scrolling through his old emails.

He finally closes out his email and opens his text messages, composing a quick note to Ellie. Scratching his head, he wonders what to write.

We missed you today. Try not to stay away too long this time.

9

Two hours later, Derek is finally almost home. His job can be demanding, but the insurance company that he works for lets him set his hours most of the time. His charming personality is perfect for his job as a broker. Usually, he is a motivated and terrific salesman, but sometimes, like this evening, the job can be draining. The last couple of hours were spent courting a potential customer only to realize way too late that he was dealing with an indecisive lead, someone who will take months to close the deal. He doesn't have time for people who don't know what they want at work or in life. He'd rather just tell you what you want.

The floodlights on the side of his house turn on, illuminating the driveway as he parks his Mustang outside of the garage. Eventually he'll get around to finding the time to clean out the garage so he can start parking in it before winter. There's nothing worse than scraping ice off the windshield on a dark, cold morning. The car door echoes in the night as he slams it shut, shattering the quiet stillness of the street. Tomorrow's schedule runs through his mind as he walks down the driveway to retrieve the mail.

His mailbox sits at the edge of the yard, facing a road that is desperately in need of another streetlight. The hinges on the box squeak in protest as he pries it open. Sliding his hand in the box, he feels around, no mail. His fingers graze the edge of something small and square, too small to be a letter or card. Trash, most likely. He grabs it and walks back toward the garbage cans, but as he lifts the lid to throw it in, the flood light catches the object, and he sees what's in his hand: a matchbook.

Weird. He didn't put it in there, and it doesn't seem likely that the mailman would have dropped it by accident, but then again, stranger things have happened. He turns the matchbook over under the light, a nondescript red square with a fresh strip on the back. No business or restaurant logo to be found. With a shake of his head, he opens the lid of the trash can, tosses the matches in, ready to get inside the house and finally eat dinner.

Waiting to leap into his arms before the door is even closed is Moose, his dog. A light brown terrier mix, Moose is Derek's world. His eyes light up from the comfort of Moose's greeting. Strangely, Moose isn't one for barking, but his nails clack across the hardwood floor as he races off toward his food dish, grunting all the way.

"Alright, boy. I know, I know." Derek grabs a can of wet food from the pantry, barely able to finish dumping it into Moose's bowl before the dog has lapped it all up. Satisfied with his meal, Moose trots back into the living room, settling down on his plush dog bed next to the recliner.

After an unappealing microwave meal and too much time spent on the couch watching the news, Derek showers and takes his tired body to bed.

Covered in a sheen of sweat, his dreams startle him awake. His fingers clumsily slide across his nightstand, knocking over an old water bottle before connecting with his phone. The brightness of the screen is blinding, and he waits for his eyes to adjust. 2:48 AM.

The dream rushes back to him vividly and he drops the phone. *His tennis shoes; clunky and dirty, planted firmly on the dust covered, rotting wooden floor. Sirens fill the air, interrupting the noise surrounding him. In one hand, a single match, in the other, the box it came in. He shoves the box in his pocket and stares at the solitary, unlit match for just a moment before it falls from his hand to the floor. Run.*

The red matchbook sitting in his garbage can outside springs to his mind, but that has nothing to do with this dream or that night, he thinks. Still, he is unsettled and there won't be any going back to sleep tonight. A shudder creeps down his spine; he's worked hard to put all of that out of his head, only for it to pop back up now, in his dreams.

A strong, sweet smell fills the kitchen as the coffee pot burbles and percolates. Derek pours himself a cup and grabs a bottle of creamer from the fridge. He settles down at the kitchen table, scrolling through his phone, switching from one social media account to the next, more out of habit than to actually look at what's happening on the internet. After some deliberation, he pulls up his text messages, finding the group text from yesterday morning, but he can't bring himself to type. They didn't know everything about his time in the Doris house and he just can't put his secret out there like that. He couldn't begin to imagine what they would think if he told them what he did that night. Or what he almost did.

Moose's collar rattles as he stands and shakes himself, coming into the kitchen to rest at his owner's feet.

The coffee burns Derek's throat as he chokes on it. *The snake in Whitney's car. The matchbook. There's no way it could be connected to each other or the house, could it?* A little bit of excitement mixed with fear washes over him; these things could bring his friends back together, closer than ever, even Ellie. But, explaining the matchbook is out of the question; that would make certain that their friendship will be torn apart forever. They could never understand, and there's no way to explain the matchbook without telling them everything. It's best to just let it go and find another way to deal with things. Every one of them became different people after being in that house. That closeness they shared had suddenly vanished. If the matchbook represents his secret from that night, then his friends must have their secrets too. It's the only explanation as to why they stopped talking. It's why he stopped. It was the singular moment that he became afraid of himself, of what he was so very close to doing. They went into the house as four best friends, but they left as individuals who no longer knew how to be around each other.

If he could just find out what their secrets are.

They're all hiding something; they wouldn't have split up otherwise. No one has wanted to talk about what they did. His mind whirls trying to work through exactly where everyone was that night, but he just can't recall. They all went off in separate rooms to explore; that much he remembers. He was so focused on his plan; it was like someone else was in his mind pushing him to do what he almost did. The thought of losing control made him want to do things that he never thought himself capable of. It seemed so perfect; they would rush back to find him and escape together, huddled up in the woods to watch the flames soar through the house, and be bonded for life. Bonded by fear and survival. That's not how things happened though, and it's for the best. But, he can't help but wonder if they would still be friends, had things gone his way.

Coffee sloshes from his mug as Moose jumps to attention, bumping into the chair, his ears stand up straight. A thick odor rises in the air, and for a moment, in his sleep deprived state, Derek thinks he must have made the coffee too strong. Only when Moose tears off to the back door, pawing at it, does Derek realize what the smell is. He pushes the curtain aside to peek out into the backyard. *Fire.* His tool shed in the backyard is on fire.

Smoke curls in giant gray tendrils as a slow burning fire snakes up from the corner of the shed. It must have just started as it hasn't engulfed the whole structure yet. Bottles of cleaning supplies fall to the bottom of the cabinet as Derek clumsily shoves them aside reaching for his extinguisher.

Angry, orange flames lick the side of his wooden shed, hungry to flourish and spread, and for just a moment, Derek pauses. In awe, he stands, watching the small fire grow bigger as it begins to take hold and slide up the wall. Moose jumps into him, knocking him off balance and out of his stupor, and he rushes outside to unload the extinguisher, putting out the small blaze. Crackles from the fire fade into silence and dirty foam drips to the ground. Derek stands still, the roar of adrenaline buzzing in his ears. The snap of a twig breaks the trance. It smells like a bonfire. Moose leads the charge toward the woods, suddenly stopping, causing Derek to trip and fall to the ground. He stands and looks around, wiping the dirt from his hands onto his sweatpants.

Surrounded only by trees and branches, there is no sign of anyone having run through here. A slight breeze blows through; leaves trickle off their trees all around him. Any footprints would be concealed by the fallen leaves and the darkness.

10

"Ow!" Whitney jumps back, dropping the scalding hot hair straightener in the sink. She sucks on her burning finger for a moment, nursing the wound. Her half-straightened, half curly, blonde locks reflect back to her in the mirror, and she decides she's over it. The cord falls to the floor as she rips the plug from the wall.

"Mommy!" Melody calls out.

Quickly, Whitney grabs a hair tie and tosses her messy hair into a low bun and rushes from the bathroom. It'll have to do.

"Oh, sweetheart! Let me help." The scene she walks into in the kitchen is pitiful and adorable all at once. Milk drips from the kitchen table as Melody struggles to try to pour it into her cereal, the large jug wobbling precariously in her tiny hands. Some mornings, actually some days are like this—putting one fire out after another. But Whitney's life would be so empty without the chaos.

Her daughter eats her breakfast, legs swinging underneath her chair, as Whitney mops up the sticky milk. She tosses the soaked paper towels in the trash before grabbing a yogurt from the fridge and ripping into it hungrily.

Guilt washes over her. She was supposed to go to grocery shop yesterday and she forgot. Now the fridge sits in its corner of the kitchen, all but empty, and Whitney has such a busy day ahead of her. It's inventory day. The department store at the mall where she works is one of those large chain stores carrying everything from housewares and toys to men's suits and makeup. She usually works in the Misses department, but she's been at the store so long, there isn't an inch of that place left that she hasn't worked at some point. Today, they are starting inventory in her current department, and most of the team will be there, which reminds her-- she left her name tag in the kitchen last night. She grabs it from the junk bowl on the counter and fastens it to her soft yellow sweater before snatching up her purse and Melody's book bag and tossing them over by the front door.

"Alright hon, time to go! We're going to be late!"

"Mommy! I haven't brushed my teeth yet!" Her daughter says in between crunches.

"Ok. Put your bowl in the sink and go do it. I'll put our stuff in the car, meet me outside."

Juggling both bags and her keys, Whitney steps outside. Thick autumn fog blankets the small neighborhood, and she shivers in the early morning chill. Her old, green Camry sits parked in the driveway, waiting to be filled with the two of them and all of their things. She hits the unlock button, the beeps interrupting the quiet solitude of the neighborhood in the morning.

A brown cardboard box resting on the hood of the car grabs Whitney's attention, and she hurries over to it, tossing the bags in the backseat before grabbing the mystery package. She takes a look at the townhomes around her; everyone is probably either still sleeping or getting ready as there's no one else outside. Perhaps one of them left a gift for her or her daughter. Gently, she opens the box and lifts the object out, a house. A small ceramic house. The cardboard box it came in left forgotten on top of the car as she turns the house around in her hands; it's about the size of a music box, but it resembles a dollhouse. It must be a gift for Melody though it doesn't appear new. Possibly from Mrs. Morgan down the street. The older woman has a soft spot for Mel, always bringing her treats during the holidays.

That's odd. Mrs. Morgan has never left anything on her car. She normally comes to the door when she has something for Melody, and when they aren't home, she leaves her trinkets on the porch.

Upon closer look, she notices the front has a small, dirty, white door with little rusty silver hinges on the side. With one hand, and carefully, as not to break it, she pops the tiny door open and leans forward, peeking inside. With a cry, she drops the house, shards scattering across the pavement. The only part of it left unbroken are two of the figurines; one male, one female, glued together at their stomachs and pressed against a shattered remnant of a peeling brown wall. A familiar looking brown wall.

Just then, the front door flies open and Melody bounces down the driveway toward the car.

"Oh! A Box! Is it a present, mommy?" The little girl spots the package forgotten on top of the car and sprints over to it.

"No! Melody, honey, go back to the door. Wait inside for me, please." Positioning herself in front of the figurines lying on the ground, Whitney tries desperately to keep her voice light. She doesn't want to frighten her daughter or inspire her curiosity. "Mommy just needs to clean up her mess!"

A car door slams, shattering the quiet morning, and Whitney whips around on her heels. "Is someone there?" The fog is much too thick and she squints but sees no one in their yards or driveways yet. Desperate to get rid of the broken dollhouse before anyone else sees it, she drops to the ground shoveling pieces into her arms. Her knee crunches on a bit of ceramic, scraping her skin and bringing tears to her eyes, but she continues trying to clean the broken pieces. An engine revs, and her head shoots up, eyes darting in every direction. But all she can see through the misty morning is the blurred red tail lights as an unrecognizable car sails down the street right past her house.

***

"Are you sure you didn't leave anything on my car, because Derek, if you did, it isn't funny. It's awful." Back home after calling in sick to work and dropping Melody off at school, Whitney paces the kitchen floor, trying her hardest not to dissolve into hysterics on the phone with Derek. Her boss was obviously unhappy, but there is no way she would be able to make it through work with this on her mind. This little ceramic house is the house—the Doris house. It's obvious. She tried calling Jackson first, but she kept getting his voicemail. Besides, the thought of telling him that someone sent her those figurine replicas of the two of them together makes her stomach turn. *Someone knows.*

"No, Whit. Why would I put something on your car? Trust me, I would never get up that early just to drive across town and put something on a car. That's insane." He laughs for a moment, quickly stopping himself when he realizes that he received a gift as well. The matchbook. *The matches, the fire, oh, God.* So, he was right about the matches and the snake being intentional.

"Well, if you didn't, who did?"

"What was it again?" He asks.

"Just a small ceramic house with figurines inside. But, I'm telling you it looked just like *the* house." Her sigh crackles on the line.

"Where were the figurines at, what were they doing?" His voice trembles, and he coughs, trying to cover it.

"Nothing, it's not important. I just need to know where it came from." Exhausted from the morning's stress, she sits down hard on the chair at the kitchen table. The line goes quiet for several seconds. "Derek, you still there?"

"Yeah. I'm just—I want to see it. Can you send me a picture?" He clears his throat.

"No, um, it's broken. I accidentally dropped it when I realized what it was. It's exactly what I'm telling you, I swear. Whoever did it set it up to look like a gift."

"Look, I got something too, a present like you, I guess. I didn't realize that's what it was at first but it makes sense. It was left in my mailbox."

"You did? What was it?" She yells.

"We can talk about it later. Let me text Jackson and Ellie; we can meet up and see which of them are playing pranks." As the words leave his lips, he thinks of the others, wondering if anything has happened to them or if he can trust any of them anymore, while Whitney is wondering the same thing about him.

When he calls back an hour later to let her know that he finally got ahold of Jackson, she is relieved. Being in her home by herself has her so afraid that she was about to hop back in her car and drive around just to get away. Someone brought this to her house; they know where she lives and what car she drives. They could be out there right now, watching her. A nervous flutter tickles her stomach. The plan is for them to meet up at Jackson's. She hasn't been there before; the last time she visited Jackson where he lived, it was a single-bed dorm room on campus with a mattress and desk and not much else. She's been to his place loads of times before, but that was always his parent's house in high school or his dorm in college, never his own home. Smiling to herself, she wonders if he ever graduated from the bean bag chairs tossed onto the floor.

"Ow!" She looks down, dropping the figurines that she has been clutching in her hand ever since she got back from taking Mel to school. Fat drops of blood drip onto the kitchen counter; the jagged edge of a broken piece of ceramic has left behind a small gash in her hand.

After cleaning out her cut and bandaging her hand, she wraps up the figurines in a paper towel and carries them to her bedroom. Soft drizzle starts to tap at her window, and for a moment, she thinks how wonderful it would be to crawl back into her bed and sleep to the sounds of the rain, not worrying about that stupid, old house. But, she has to meet up with everyone in thirty minutes, and she has no idea how Derek convinced Ellie to come, so she'd better show up as well.

She rummages around in her closet for a moment before finally pulling out an old, yellow tin coin bank. A relic from her childhood. Turning it around in her hands, she remembers how she used to love the multicolored hot air balloons painted on it—she was obsessed with them as a child. Back when her biggest worry was what Santa would bring her or who would sit with her at lunch. The lid sticks a little from age, but she tugs it off and tucks the awful little gift inside before burying the whole thing deep in the back of her closet. There is no way she is showing that to anyone today, not even Jackson.

In her rush to get out the door, her knee knocks painfully against the coffee table. With a yelp, she clutches her knee, noticing Melody's latest school project still resting on top of the table; a big red-letter A scrawled in the top corner. She pauses, staring at it. A colorful counting caterpillar for her math class. The caterpillar reminds Whitney of the snake in her car, which all of a sudden doesn't seem like much of a freak-accident anymore.

11

The car kicks up dust while Ellie speeds down the long dirt road to Jackson's house. She chuckles to herself. Boredom has her coming all the way out in the country just for social interaction with people who thought nothing of dropping her friendship so long ago. The thought makes her miss life in Minneapolis, before quickly realizing she no longer has any friends left there either, not after what happened.

When they were in high school, Jackson lived in a house on the edge of town, out in the country, but this place is even more secluded. Nothing but woods and pine trees line the sides of the one lane road, blurring into each other as she glances at them from her window. Finally, she reaches the sprawling house and is amazed by the simple, yet beautiful craftsmanship of it.

She pulls in behind Derek's Mustang. *Obnoxious.* There's a green Camry parked beside Jackson's truck and she assumes that it belongs to Whitney—she must have traded in her zippy little car from college for something more kid friendly. Ellie is the last to arrive, but she's not bothered. She has no problems with making them wait. Her faithful Mazda idles as she procrastinates, nervous about seeing everyone.

To ease the nerves a bit before going inside, she takes out her phone. The Facebook app loads, and she scrolls through absentmindedly before switching over to LinkedIn. She pulls up her profile page to read over her resume again, but something's different. An icy tendril of fear snakes down her neck. *This can't be right.* She reads through once more in disbelief, the phone trembling in her hand. There was no way she was going to add her last job on her page in the event that a potential employer might call asking about her, but right there it is. Listed under past positions, it clearly reads; **Morgan Furniture—Junior Designer**. And just under that is written; **Reason for leaving—termination due to harassment**.

A sense of dread washes over her; she didn't write those words. She never mentioned Morgan Furniture at all on her resume. In fact, after she was fired, she vowed to herself never to speak of the place again. Someone wrote it. Someone who was able to get into her account. The rain picks up and fat drops beat down on the hood of her car, and she suddenly feels very exposed. All alone even though her old friends are just inside the house. There might as well be miles between them. There's a feeling of someone watching her, waiting for her reaction, but that can't be. Her hand slides to the gear shifter, ready to turn tail and run. But she remembers the sound of Derek's voice and the urgency of his phone call, and she wonders what he could possibly want that's so important. *Were they hacked as well?*

Her fingers move swiftly as she taps the edit button on her page. Just a quick delete and then she'll go inside. She'll worry about her mysterious hacker when she gets back to the motel. The moment she taps the button, the screen refreshes. The app must have restarted; the login page appears. **Incorrect Password** shows on the screen. She tries several more times, but it's no use. She's been locked out of her account with her altered resume out there in cyberspace for all to see. Angrily, she beats the phone against the steering wheel. By now who knows how many potential employers have looked at this. Resignation finally sets in; at this point, there is nothing to be done but to wipe the tears from her eyes, square her shoulders, and go inside. She will have to deal with it later.

The doorbell chimes a little melody in the large farmhouse. Without an excess of furniture to pad the noise, it carries eerily throughout the space. Derek, Jackson, and Whitney are all seated around the rarely used dining table, barely speaking to one another. Unable to control herself; Whitney jumps up as the doorbell rings. "I'll get it."

The noise is a welcome break to the awkwardness that has settled over the waiting group.

"Hi El, come on in." So preoccupied with her own worries, Whitney doesn't even notice the blotchy, tear-streaked face of her former friend. She doesn't wait for Ellie to remove her coat before making her way back into the dining room.

"Nice to see you too." Ellie mutters under her breath and tosses her coat across the couch. She hurries after Whitney, confused at her lack of usual bubbliness, and finds the three of them seated around the table looking as miserable as she feels. Well, except for Jackson. His golden-brown eyes are laser-focused on Whitney. *That torch must still burn bright.*

"Ellie! I'm so glad you made it." Derek jumps out of his seat and grabs her by the arm, leading her to the table.

"Uh, me too." She follows along, confused by his sudden excitement to see her. She sits opposite him and studies his face. His normally vibrant green eyes now dull and tinged red. He looks frightened. *Like a caged animal ready to run the instant the door swings open.*

All those things he was rambling on about over the phone--and now her tampered resume, something similar must've happened to him. It's clear that something strange is going on. Nausea flows through her insides; what if someone got into her motel room and put those spiders in her bed? *Has something just as awful happened to him?*

"Hey, El." Jackson finally speaks, the spell Whitney has over him broken, for the moment.

"So, what's up? Why call me here like this, I've got a lot of work—"

"We all have work to do." Whitney suddenly snaps. Whoever is pulling pranks is now messing with her livelihood—her job, and her ability to provide for her daughter.

"Yes, but it can wait." Derek tries to diffuse the tension. "We need to figure some things out."

"What are you talking about?" Ellie twists her long, dark hair around in her hands, squeezing the rain water from it. She figures playing dumb is the best route. Let them talk first; then, she can decide how much to disclose.

"Well…" Scratching at his ear, Derek tries to figure out how to say what he needs to say without telling everything. "So, I don't know if you know yet, but someone bought the house."

"Someone bought your house? I don't know what this-"

"No. The Doris house, Ellie." His eyes search her face but she gives no reaction. "Anyway, someone has bought the house. Whitney and I saw the sign in the yard, and then, I don't know. Something strange happened, not just to me, but also Whitney. Could just be coincidence but…"

"It's not." Whitney interrupts.

"What happened?" Ellie's voice is hard, but she shivers noticeably, remembering the feel of the spiders crawling on her skin.

"I thought the snake in my car must've got in on its own, but now I'm not sure." Whitney says.

"What! There was a snake in your car?" Ellie yells. "Why did I not know this?"

"You haven't been coming around. You've barely responded to my texts." Whitney answers quietly.

Heat rises to Ellie's cheeks. She wonders if she's holding too tightly to her grudges. They're all adults now; maybe it's time to let it go. She can still guard herself but forgive her friends; they do seem to be making an effort. But, a little voice in the back of her mind worries they are only talking to her because of what's going on. "I'm sorry about that. I've been busy, but I'm here now."

"Anyway," Derek interrupts the moment. "Whit got a weird package this morning and I've had some things happen as well."

"What things? What kind of package?" Ellie whirls around in her seat to face him.

"Oh, nothing. I don't—just something happened. I'm not really ready to say." He still can't bring himself to come clean with his demons. Running his hands through his shiny brown hair, his eyes plead with her not to force it. That side of him has been locked away for years, and he certainly doesn't want to shine a light on it now.

"I suppose I can join the club then because if that's what it is—the house, then it got me too."

"What do you mean?" Whitney asks.

Ellie tucks a strand of hair behind her ear; she tells them about the spiders in her motel bed but leaves out the recent addition to her resume. It's no one's business what went on in Minneapolis.

"You've been awfully quiet. What are you thinking?" Derek raises an eyebrow at Jackson.

Twisting his calloused hands, Jackson pops his knuckles and looks into the eyes of each of his friends. "Nothing. I mean, it just sounds silly. You guys had a couple of weird things happen—even though you won't share all of them." He locks his gaze on Derek. "And you say it's not a coincidence, but maybe it is because nothing has happened to me, and I was at that house as well. Are you guys sure it isn't just random bad luck? A snake in the car, I mean it *could* happen, same with the spiders."

"No." Whitney whispers, barely audible.

"What?" Jackson asks.

"No! There's no way it's an accident. Sure, at first, I thought so too, but now, someone sent me something specifically about that house. Today. It's why I'm here and not at work." Whitney's cheeks flush, embarrassed at having raised her voice. "Maybe it's not the house; maybe it's someone who saw us inside of the house."

"I was sent something too." Derek adds. "And before you ask, I'd really rather not talk about it."

"But why not you?" Ellie turns to Jackson, eyebrows raised. "I mean all of these things happen to us and not to you, kinda odd isn't it?"

Three pairs of eyes turn to Jackson. He shakes his head. "I don't know. What I do know is, we can't figure out what is happening and how to fix it if you guys won't say what's going on. You can't just tell me you were sent something and not say what it was."

Whitney kicks his leg under the table, shutting him up. Their friends probably wouldn't care now that they hooked up, but they would be angry that after all this time neither Whitney nor Jackson told them.

"Besides, that night wasn't the first time we were there. Remember senior year? We went to the house then and nothing happened." Jackson returns Ellie's stare.

"We didn't go inside then." Whitney's mouth settles into a thin line.

"All I'm saying is everyone used to go in there; why would anyone care about us?" Jackson sighs.

"Well, I need to use your bathroom." Slamming her hands on the table, Ellie stands, following the direction Jackson points to down the hallway.

"Bathroom's down the hall to the right. Anyone want more coffee?"

Derek and Whitney both nod and follow Jackson into his kitchen.

The light is already on in the bathroom, making it easy for Ellie to find. She shakes her hair out and stares in the mirror for a few seconds before washing her hands in the sink. The hot water burns her skin as if she could burn away the past couple of days. Feeling more settled, she turns off the taps and leaves, closing the door behind her. Even if just for a few seconds, she had to get away and breathe. She won't be pressured into talking about how her anger took hold of her that night. Or how it's happened once more since then.

Hushed whispers echo from the kitchen; she turns her head the other way. The hallway is long and stretches the length of the rest of the house. She could go join the group in the kitchen, or she could turn right and explore the inner workings of Jackson's home just a little bit. Curiosity wins and she silently moves down the dark hallway. Rain beats down harder on the roof, and she wishes she was back in her cozy apartment in Minneapolis curled up with a book. There's a small door to her left, and she opens it revealing a simple, almost bare linen closet. Truly a bachelor, the only items the closet holds are one blanket and a couple of towels. Moving along, there is another door just past the closet. She flings the door open, hoping to find his bedroom, but what she finds is even better, his office. Her shoes squeak slightly as she turns on her heel to peer down the hallway, making sure everyone is still huddled in the kitchen before stepping inside.

His linen closet may be bare, but he has definitely taken some time in his office. A large roll-top desk is pushed against a beautiful, white-framed arched window. Seven-foot book shelves are placed on either side of the window. It's a gorgeous office except for the walls. Ellie has never liked wood-paneled walls; they have always given her the creeps, like something out of a bad seventies' horror film. The walls here are no exception.

The urge to snoop is too powerful to ignore, so she runs to the door, peeks outside and seeing no one in the hallway, rushes back to rifle through Jackson's desk. The cabinets hold lots of file folders bulging with blue prints and pages covered in numbers she doesn't understand. Only a stapler, ruler, and a few pencils rest inside the single drawer. Disappointed, she turns, looking around the room. The books and accordion organizers on his bookshelves hold nothing of intrigue, and there's no other furniture except for a couple of sitting chairs and an empty coffee table. No one could ever accuse Jackson of being a hoarder.

Ellie gives the room one more quick look-over before turning toward the door, but then she remembers something. She studies the desk again. As a little girl, she once had a roll-top desk similar to this one, only hers wasn't solid oak. Her dad found it for her at a yard sale and she was obsessed with it, doing all of her reading and writing at that desk. It made her feel important—especially when she found that small hidden shelf at the top just under the lid.

Her ears on high alert, she listens for anyone coming down the hallway. After all, she has been gone a long time now. That doesn't stop her from quickly moving back across the room and shoving her hand up behind the roll-top. There it is, the secret ledge. It can't be seen by looking underneath.

You just have to feel for it, but the ledge stretches the length of the desk, and she slides her palm across it until she makes contact with something. Her hand shakes as she pulls out some rolled up papers, excited about finding a secret.

Hungrily, she reads through the documents: a typed home purchase offer, and a house listing. A strangled cry escapes her throat—she knows this address. This offer is for the Doris house. Derek and Whitney need to see this. Quickly, she reaches in her back pocket for her phone. *Dammit!* Her phone is still in her coat pocket back in the living room.

The pages flutter to the ground as Ellie sinks to her knees, not understanding why the papers she just saw are hidden in Jackson's home. *Is he buying the house?*

With trembling hands, she carefully folds them the way they were and replaces everything on the secret shelf before tearing out of the room. The door shuts behind her and she charges up the hallway bumping right into Jackson just outside of the dining room. A small smile rests on his lips.

"Ellie! Is everything okay? We were starting to worry. I was just coming to check on you." Jackson grabs her shoulders, looking her in the eyes.

"I'm fine." She stammers. "I just—I have to go. I've got some work that needs to get done."

"Yeah, but we still need to talk about this."

"Yeah." Derek appears around the corner with his coffee, steam rising from the top. "We still don't know what's going on."

Ellie looks from Derek to Jackson, feeling cornered. "Well, when you figure it out, let me know." With that, she snatches her coat and stumbles to the front door, tripping over her feet the whole way to her car.

From her rearview mirror, she sees the group crowding the door, watching her. She wishes she could tell Derek and Whitney what she saw, but she can't with Jackson so close, so she does the only thing she can. She hits the gas and tries to leave the fear in her wake.

12

"I'm telling you what I saw." Ellie wraps her hands around her hot chai, warming them up in the cold air. The rain has finally died off, and the clouds have parted to leave behind a beautiful, cold and clear night. After several unsettling hours alone in her motel room, she couldn't take it anymore. She had to tell someone about the papers in Jackson's office, so she gave in and called Whitney, asking her to meet up at Lake Shore. It's a little chilly to be having this conversation at their table outside, but the chairs have dried off, and she doesn't want anyone to overhear.

"But it doesn't make any sense, El. Why would Jackson even want to buy that house? He already has a home, one that he built practically by himself!" Whitney's eyes grow large and wild, imploring Ellie to be wrong on this. Even though seeing Jackson in person brought that same butterfly feeling back from so long ago, her judgment doesn't feel clouded. It's just not something that he would do. Nine years wouldn't change him that drastically. "You must have read it wrong; he probably just has a contract to do some work over there or something."

"I didn't read it wrong. I wish I had, but I didn't; it was a purchase offer. Why do you think I left so fast? I couldn't even look at him." A wave of pity settles deep into her heart: she knows how much Whitney doesn't want it to be true, but it's not something that she could keep inside to spare anyone's feelings.

"But you could've asked him about it." Whitney picks at a chip in her nail polish.

"Are you kidding? After what's happened! I mean, the spiders were bad enough, but Whitney..." She stops herself, shaking her head. She doesn't want to get into the resume thing. Once she opens that door, she could lose all credibility. There's no way to explain her side of it without coming off as crazy.

Whitney's hand covers Ellie's on the table. "What is it? What else happened?"

For a moment, Ellie just stares at her old friend; she wishes so badly that she could confide in her the way that she used to. They were supposed to be best friends all those years ago, but Whitney ditched her after that night, and Ellie just let her go. She wasn't going to try to force the friendship back together the way that Derek had. That wasn't the way she worked. It would feel so good to open up, but the trust isn't there yet. "It's not important. What I'm worried about is whether or not Jackson is the one buying the house. If you don't believe it, go have a look for yourself. It's all right there in his desk."

The bell over the exit door jingles as someone steps outside of the coffee shop, casting a shadow over their table. Ellie turns to see a tall, incredibly attractive man standing under the shop's cast iron lantern by the door, tucking his wallet into the back pocket of his dark jeans. Heat rushes to her face, and she swivels back in her chair when he looks up, catching her stare. She fiddles with her paper cup, trying to play it off, but his footsteps grow louder behind them, stopping only once he reaches their table.

"Ellie Meechum, is that you?"

Her cup forgotten, she looks up into the softest brown eyes. "Um, yeah. I'm sorry, have we met?"

His eyes crinkle at the corners when he smiles. "Oh, yeah, sorry. James. We went to Northwest together. James Myer." His gaze breaks from Ellie. "Whitney Parker, I thought that might be you. Wow. Ya'll look exactly the same. Seriously, you haven't changed a bit."

"Hi." Whitney smiles politely, searching his face in

hopes of remembering him.

"James Myer." Ellie says to herself. Her brain whirls through her memories of classmates, trying to place him. It hits her and she giggles, remembering the skinny kid who sat behind her in band class. His instrument was almost bigger than him. "James, tuba, right?"

"That's me, except I play professionally now." He smiles proudly.

"Oh wow! Are you serious?"

"No." Smirking, his gaze flicks from Ellie to Whitney and back to Ellie. His lips curl up into a devilish smile that sends bubbles fizzing throughout Ellie's stomach.

Ellie rolls her eyes, and Whitney laughs, suddenly remembering James. He looks nothing like the guy who spent all of 11th grade desperately trying to hang out with their group. He was so plain back then, almost forgettable, if not for the fact that he still looked like a middle-schooler. But, standing there in front of them in a fitted, beige thermal shirt, it's obvious he has grown taller, more muscular.

She recalls the time that he stopped by their lunch table, short and gawky, awkwardly asking the four if they wanted to hang out after school. Reluctantly, they agreed, but then became so wrapped up in their own dramas, they forgot, leaving him stranded without a ride in the school parking lot. Later that night when they'd gathered back at Derek's house, Jackson remembered, and they all got a good laugh out of it. Whitney never told them that she had remembered much earlier and had driven back to school only to find he had already gone. They would have teased her endlessly if they'd known how bad it made her feel.

Propelled by her old guilt, Whitney smiles a little too big at him. "It's great to see you again, James. What have you been up to?"

"Oh, you know. Just working. That sort of thing."

"What kind of work—?" Whitney starts, her voice fades as he interrupts.

"How about you guys though, married yet? Kids?" He runs his hands through his thick, dark hair.

"No marriages, but this one has a little girl." Ellie

points to Whitney.

"Oh, yeah?"

"Melody. She's five and a total mess." Whitney smiles at the thought of her daughter.

"That's really great to hear. I'm sure she is beautiful, just like her mother. Listen—" His phone buzzes loudly in his pocket. He takes it out to check, backing away to answer the call.

"Can you believe it? That's James Myer," Ellie whispers.

Whitney leans close to the table. "Seriously, when did he grow up? I didn't even recognize him. And how come we all look the same, and he got to grow into that! Oh my God, do you remember…"

"Yes!" Ellie squeals, her hesitation forgotten as she laughs with Whitney. She was never one to apologize or wallow in guilt.

Finished with his call, James shoves his phone in his pocket and returns to the table, both women desperately trying to stifle their laughter.

"It was so nice running into you guys. But listen, I've got to go. Maybe we can all catch up sometime." He tilts his head flirtatiously, and his eyes sparkle under the lantern. "Ya'll still see Derek and Jackson?"

"Um, yeah. Sometimes." Whitney answers while Ellie stares at her shoes, trying to avoid the lure of his gaze.

"Well, great! Let's all get together soon."

"Sure." Both women speak at the same time.

He quickly moves around their table, heading out but squeezing Ellie's shoulder as he goes. Her eyes shoot up to him, wide as saucers. "Bye!" She calls.

"What was that!" Whitney giggles at her moonstruck friend.

"Seriously, that could not have been skinny tuba kid, James Myer."

"Right!" They both double over once again. Contentment settles deep into Whitney's heart; this silly run-in is just what the two of them needed to begin repairing their friendship. It's a start. If only this weird thing with Jackson was cleared up.

Ellie settles down, wiping tears of laughter from her eyes. Her tone quickly becoming more serious. "But really, Whitney. What should we do about Jackson? You know we can't just leave it."

"We could always just ask him." Whitney frowns.

Ellie rolls her eyes. "Oh yeah, okay. Should I say; 'Hi Jackson, I was snooping around your office and found a purchase offer for that creepy house we all broke into, and oh, you wouldn't happen to be the one who put spiders in my bed would you?'"

"You're right." Sighing, Whitney asks; "So, what then? We don't mention it? What about Derek? Do we tell him?"

"I guess we should. But he's being shady too. He says something happened to him, although he isn't saying what it was. So, I don't know."

"None of us are really saying." Whitney reminds her. "Let's talk to Derek before we do anything else. It might help to know if whatever happened was something he thinks Jackson would do." Whitney picks at her fingernails, hiding the shake in her hands.

"Alright then. Let's go." Ellie snatches up her keys and purse. "I'll drive."

"You want to do this now? It's getting late and I've got to get Mel soon." Whitney asks.

"Why not? I'd rather do something than sit around waiting for the next awful thing to happen. We won't be long."

A strand of hair falls in Whitney's eyes as she stands, and she brushes it aside. "Alright. Mel's at my mom's; just let me call real quick and see if she can stay the night, it's already almost her bedtime." She walks away, phone in hand, before Ellie has a chance to respond.

"Okay. Let's do it." Whitney walks back to the table, tucking her phone in her purse, determination on her face.

13

The frenzied pounding at the front door kicks Derek's adrenaline into overdrive. His laptop falls to the floor as he jumps from the couch, hurrying to check the peephole. Relieved, he lets out a deep breath. It's just Whitney and Ellie. But, if they're here this late and together, then something has to be wrong. From the strange way that Ellie ran away from Jackson's earlier today, this must be important.

"Hey, what are you guys doing here? Everything okay?" He opens the door wide, letting the women in. Moose races into the room, jumping and sniffing at his new visitors. His nose eagerly pushes into Ellie's leg, hoping for a playmate, but settling for a scratch behind the ears.

"We need to talk to you." Ellie answers. Moose paws at her leg to continue. Once he realizes she's no longer focused on him, he moves on to Whitney for a petting before trotting back to his bed to dramatically plop back down.

"Well, Ellie saw something at Jackson's earlier. We thought you should know about it." Whitney walks further into the room, coming to rest at the oversized beige couch. She spots the laptop open on the floor, her own Facebook page lighting up the screen.

"What's this?" She holds up the laptop for both to see.

Red hot embarrassment blooms across Derek's cheeks. "Oh, nothing. I was just browsing around Facebook."

He snatches the computer from her hands, quickly closing it. It's better if she thinks he has a little crush than let them know he was trying to keep tabs on them.

Ellie shivers, wondering if he was stalking around on Whitney's Facebook page, could he also have been looking at her own LinkedIn account? She decides to revisit that later; this thing with Jackson is far too important. *Unless he already knows about the offer.* His reaction to the news should tell her what she needs to know.

"Sit down." Derek motions to the furniture. "Can I get ya'll something?"

"No thanks, we just came from the coffee shop." Ellie takes a seat on the armchair closest to the front door. She studies the living room; the hunter green accent wall, and the dark abstract painting above the fireplace suggests that his tastes have drastically changed over the past decade. She expected a tower of beer cans on an IKEA coffee table. Instead, the one before her is metal and glass and completely smudge free.

"Actually, I'd love a water." Whitney says as she settles down onto the couch, still glancing at the closed laptop on the table.

"You got it." In the kitchen the single serve coffee percolates and fills his cup, as he grabs a bottle of water from the fridge for Whitney. Drinks in hand, he starts back into the living room but he stops when he hears whispering. Leaning against the wall and balancing the cup and bottle, Derek overhears the two chuckling and chatting about their night. His mouth drops as he hears them mention James. It's been ages since he has seen James Meyer, but he can plainly remember how much he hated that kid. The way Ellie seems to be almost gushing, she must have a thing for the guy now. *Great. Just what I need, James hanging around again.*

"So what's so important you guys had to talk to me tonight?" Barging in and interrupting the conversation; Derek tosses Whitney her water as he sits across from her. The air of humor is quickly replaced with a sense of doom as things shift back to the serious topic they wish they didn't have to discuss.

A hint of hesitation nudges Ellie, but she has to tell

someone else; otherwise, they might never get to the truth. With a few deep breaths to calm her nerves, she launches into the story of how she came to find the purchase offer in Jackson's office.

"What!?"

Flinching at Derek's raised voice, at least now Ellie can tell that he genuinely had no idea what Jackson has been up to.

"I mean, it doesn't make any sense. Why wouldn't he have told me?" Derek slides his hand across his chin. His breathing is measured as he forces himself to calm down. It's Jackson's business and he doesn't need to control it.

"Why didn't he tell any of us?" Whitney wonders.

"Well, we haven't really spoken to each other much, none of us. But still, we were talking about how the house has sold and what's been happening. You would think he would mention it." Ellie shrugs. "Unless he doesn't think what's going on has anything to do with the house. He did say as much."

"But how could it not?" Derek checks his volume, pushing himself to remain calm. "What happened to me was connected to that house. There's no other explanation. Besides, maybe you guys don't talk, but he and I still do sometimes."

Ellie straightens her back, determined to ignore the slight.

"I mean, my situation was pretty obviously about the house too." Whitney nods.

"The snake?" Ellie's face crinkles in confusion.

"Well, no not that; it was something else. I'm sure the snake was there to hurt me or scare me, whatever this freak is trying to do. But, there was a ceramic replica of the house on the hood of my car this morning. Like, an exact copy."

"Are you serious?" Ellie shifts uncomfortably in her chair. "I don't know, guys. I can't tell what Jackson is thinking. Maybe he didn't think any of this was a big deal, or maybe he didn't tell us about the offer because he's the one leaving these morbid 'gifts.' Did you tell him about the model?"

"No. I didn't get the chance." It's not true. There was plenty of opportunity to bring it up; she just didn't want to have to answer any questions about what was inside. "But; he doesn't think it's a big deal because nothing has happened to him." She whispers, barely wanting to say the words.

Derek's shoulders slump. "I'm sorry El, but are you implying that Jackson had something to do with what's going on, based on a few papers? Because I'm just not buying it. I mean, come on guys, we have known him practically our whole lives; he wouldn't-"

"Wouldn't what?" Arms crossed, Ellie stares him down.

"Wouldn't do what this person did."

Whitney twists a ring around her middle finger. "Derek, you need to tell us what happened. I'm so sick of hearing that no one wants to talk about it. Whether Jackson bought the house or not, I would like to be able to get into my car without constantly checking for snakes." The fact that she, herself, doesn't want to disclose any details isn't lost on her.

His eyes close for several seconds until finally he stands and sighs. "You want to know what little present I got? Come this way. I'll show you." He leads the women through the kitchen to the back door and flips the switch for the porch light. "Go ahead, look outside."

"What is it? I don't see anything." Impatience is written all over Ellie's face.

Whitney peers out of the window; her knees buckle, and she grips the ledge. "Oh, my God. Are you kidding me? Derek, why would someone set fire to your shed?"

"I don't know," he lies.

"Derek! This is serious. What if it had spread? You could have been hurt! Your house could have caught fire! What does this have to do with the Doris house?"

"I said I don't know!" He snaps. "Someone put a snake in your car. Why was that? Or El, was it spiders you said? Why would someone load a bed down with spiders? Does that have anything to do with the house?"

"But you said there was no other explanation." Whitney presses.

Wild eyed, and clearly upset, Derek dissolves into helpless trembles. "Jackson wouldn't do this."

"Did you call the cops?" Ellie asks.

"No. I should have. But, what good would it do? It's not like whoever did it left a signature. I can handle it myself."

Ellie crosses the room and takes his arm, calming the shakes that run over his body. He pulls her into him, giving her the first real hug she's received since being back home. "If you're not ready to talk, that's alright," She says. "But it seems to me that the sale of Doris's house triggered something in someone. We haven't talked in a long time, but her house is the most likely connection between us. We need to start looking at what that could be and why. And Derek, I hate to say it, but Jackson was the only other person in that house with us."

He shakes his head, not trusting his own voice to speak.

A whimper comes from behind them. They both turn to find Whitney back on the couch, tears streaming down her cheeks. "No, not Jackson. He wouldn't." She whispers. "The house could be haunted; everyone always said it was."

"Okay." Derek says, mostly to calm himself. "I'm not convinced that it's Jackson, but Whitney, tell me if the house was haunted, why didn't anything happen the night we were in it? Why would a ghost wait until all these years later when the place is under contract to mess with us?" Derek's eyes soften, and he sits beside her.

"I know you don't want to believe that Jackson could be capable of doing these things. I don't either, but we need to come to terms with the fact that we really don't know where his head is anymore." Ellie sits on the other side of Whitney, taking her hand. "Eventually, we are going to have to start talking about what we did that night." Something dark flashes in her eyes, just for a moment. She's trying to reconcile, but memories of how things ended with all of them continuously flood her mind.

There was a day not long after they went to the house, maybe a couple of weeks later, when she saw the three of them hanging out together on campus. Wild cherries and magnolia trees had just begun to blossom, giving the college a beautiful vibrancy that it was sorely missing during the barren months of winter. The scent of the magnolias had boosted her spirits as she walked to class with a smile on her face for the first time in quite a while. Her friends had begun to drift apart in the past two weeks, but the combination of the weather and the iced coffee from the student café was doing its work to relieve her stress. The kind of day that makes you feel like the world can be yours. So what if she no longer had her boyfriend or her lifelong friends? And, so what if she was failing most of her classes; she could turn things around, she would start with not missing anymore lectures. But, as she strolled down the center path toward the foreign language building, there was Derek, Whitney, and Jackson, seated on a bench by the bookstore without her. Never would she forget the feeling of not being included, or the tears that sprang to the corners of her eyes as she ran away before they could realize she was there.

"I know what it looks like, I just can't see that in him." Whitney hiccups back her tears.

"Maybe you don't know him as well as you thought you did." Ellie mutters. "Maybe none of us know each other like we thought."

"It's late. Why don't you take me back to my car and we can talk about all of this tomorrow? Maybe things will look different in the morning." Whitney grabs her coat, not bothering to wait for Ellie's answer.

"We'll talk more then." Derek gives each a peck on the cheek as he holds the door open for them.

As soon as the door closes, he slumps down against it. He hears Ellie's car roar to life and checks the peephole to watch them as they back out of the driveway. He makes his way across the room to retrieve his laptop and settle down into the plush couch, and with a grimace, he pulls up three different Facebook profiles.

14

Ten minutes have passed since she pulled back into the coffee shop parking lot and dropped off Whitney, but Ellie is still sitting in her car. Her heart is racing, and she's more confused than ever. Regardless of what she said to Derek and Whitney, it's not easy for her to suspect Jackson the way that she does; in high school, he was like a brother to her. They teased each other, passed notes in the hallway, and he was always there when she needed advice about guys. That night at the house, she almost didn't show up. Jackson was the only reason she went.

Earlier that day she had found out that she was nearly failing out of college. Devastated, she just wanted to see Blake, her boyfriend of two years. They had met her sophomore year at the campus bookstore. He was from out of state and had come to college for the architecture program. They bonded over their mutual disdain for textbook prices. Shared grumbles in the checkout line led to lunch in the dining hall, and the rest was history. They were together from then on. He wasn't part of her group of friends and that's how she preferred it. She wanted the drama from her relationship and friendships separate; she always wanted her friends to take her side in her complaints. Those two years with Blake had changed her. She'd grown as a person. He was her first real love. He'd always had a way of making things better. Except that particular night when she showed up to his apartment to find him there with another girl, in nothing but his boxers. The girl—some tiny blonde—was stretched out like a cat on his couch, wearing his t-shirt.

Her whole world was in a tailspin; she couldn't bear to be alone, so she went with Derek's dumb idea to check out the haunted house so that she could confide in Jackson, get his helping straightening her life out. But he only had time for Whitney that night, and once they parted ways, she felt like she had lost her brother. Maybe she felt a little jealousy when she saw his hand move across Whitney's back, guiding her to a secluded room in the house, but it was only because she needed him, and right then, she needed to be more important to him than anyone else.

Mascara-stained tears run down her cheeks, but she squares her shoulders and wipes her eyes before putting the car in drive. It's time to see the house. She would never admit it, but until now, she's been afraid to go. It's no longer avoidable; something seems to pull her to the place where her friendships went to die. With the music up loud, she drives until she finds the train tracks. The car eases to the side of the road, and she hops out, walking over the tracks just like the four of them did nine years ago. There's a little group of houses on the other side of the tracks, and she wonders if they shake and rattle when a train comes through.

The sold sign lingers in the yard, but there are no lights on in the house. Nor is there a car in the driveway, so she keeps going. Gravel crunches underfoot as she makes her way up to the house. A hoot from an owl close by nearly sends her racing back to her car, but she presses on. Her foot hits the wooden step, and she hesitates, looking around. She doesn't notice the rustle of the tall bushes by the neighbor's yard or the pair of eyes watching her from behind them.

The wood on the porch is rotted and will have to be gutted; most likely the entire house will as well. It creaks loudly as she takes each step. With a trembling hand, she reaches out to turn the doorknob. The door doesn't budge. The broken lock that allowed them entry so long ago has now been replaced with a brand new one. Sighing, she retreats back down the steps. It's for the best, she tells herself, best not to go back in time that way.

***

The early morning sun washes over the house in a soft yellow. Ellie stands outside of her parent's front door wringing her hands. She's been back in town for three whole days now, and it's time she tells them before someone else sees her and does it first. Both of their cars are in the driveway. She assumed they would be. Her mother is retired, and her father works from home most Fridays.

The doorbell echoes so loudly throughout the house that she can hear it from outside. Strange, she thinks, to be ringing the doorbell of the home she spent most of her life in, but she doesn't know the protocol anymore. Could she use her key? Just walk on in? What if they thought she was an intruder?

Freezing in only a thin white sweater and jeans, she tries to stamp away the fall morning chill from her legs until finally the door swings open.

"Ellie! Sweetheart, what are you doing here? Come on, get inside!" Her mother ushers her in.

"Hi, mom. It's good to see you." She falls comfortably into her mother's hug.

"Jeff! Honey, come here. Ellie's home!" Her mother shouts down the hall.

Footsteps echo in the hallway, and before she knows it, Ellie is being swooped up into her father's embrace. "Ellie Bell! What are you doing home?" He sets her back on her feet and guides her to the living room.

Dozens of answers run through her mind; she hadn't planned what to say. She wonders if she should tell them the same story that she told her friends. In this case, she thinks, it's best to go with the least amount of information.

"Oh, I'm back for a while. Minneapolis was too far away, and my job wasn't what I expected so I came home. Just for a little while. Besides, it's almost Thanksgiving."

"But honey, I thought you loved your job." Her mother rounds the corner, handing her daughter a glass of water.

"I did at first. But it just didn't work out." Her nervous hands shake as she runs them through her hair. "So, I got a room at the motel, and I'm looking around for another job." She smiles, trying her hardest to appear nonchalant.

Her father plops down on the navy-blue sofa. "That's ridiculous honey. You'll stay here. Save your money."

"Are you sure? But, my room—"

"You can stay in the guest room; it's bigger anyway." Her mother comes to sit beside Ellie on the loveseat.

"You don't mind? I don't want to get in the way."

Shooing her comment away with his hand, her dad laughs. "Don't be silly, Ellie Bell. You're staying. I'll run out and grab your bags from the car."

"I kinda already unloaded my stuff at the motel." Ellie says.

"Well, that's alright. You go pack it up and tell them you're checking out." Her mother pats her hand.

More comfortable than she imagined; Ellie twists a strand of her long, dark hair around her finger and nods. She soaks in the calmness of her parent's home. There are few updates here and there, but mostly, it's just how she remembers with its soft gray carpet and blue couch. The floral prints on the walls are new, but the dark wooden coffee table and sideboard are exactly the same. Her lips turn up into a genuine smile, happy to be back. She missed this. The feeling of security that comes from being with her parents.

"I will in a bit. I'm happy just to sit here and rest a while."

15

A rickety wheel squeaks and wobbles as Jackson navigates the large cart down the outdoor aisles of the hardware store. He's working at Mr. Walker's house today, one of five clients that hired him for their yards in a fairly new neighborhood in town. The bags of mulch send dirt and dust flying toward his face while he drops bag after bag onto the cart. He wipes his brow with his arm and checks over the list on his phone. He still needs to get some shrubs and small trees. The customer isn't picky and left the greenery up to him, so he wanders around thinking over his options. Mr. Walker did specify absolutely no Bradford Pears. He really should have one of his guys do this part for him, he thinks. Sometimes, he pays a couple of teenage boys to help him with the big jobs, but mostly he likes to work alone. His business is small, and he prefers to keep it that way. Working with his hands is more comfortable to him than overseeing others do the job. And right now, he would much rather be out digging in the earth than shopping around.

Lost in thought over whether to use stone or concrete pavers, Jackson pays no attention to the man walking up behind him. He doesn't feel the eyes on the back of his head.

"Tough choice," says the man.

"Mhm." Jackson mumbles, turning his head to acknowledge the speaker. "Oh! Hey, James. How's it going?" He shifts his cart out of the way, smiling.

"Good, good. Got a showing this afternoon, just

trying to spruce it up a bit." He runs his hand through his dark hair, thinking back to when he ran into the girls. He didn't bother to mention to them that he's seen Jackson quite often lately. "Hey man, sorry you missed out on the Doris house; let me know when you're ready to start looking around again. When you're ready to switch realtors, we can take a look at what I've got listed."

"I'm just gonna stay where I am for now, but I'll let you know if I start looking again." He laughs.

"Sounds good. Well, I've gotta get to it. Give it some thought. I've got some great places." James claps a hand on Jackson's shoulder as he starts past.

"Will do. See ya." Jackson replies, turning back to the pavers and his decision over which to use.

James zips up his black jacket, covering the **FARMWOOD REALTY** logo emblazoned on his polo and walks through the sliding doors without making a single purchase.

With all the materials needed piled high onto his cart, Jackson makes his way to the checkout, coming to wait behind a man in painter's clothes. His mind wanders to Ellie. He hasn't heard from her since she ran out of his house in a fit. He texted her shortly after, but she didn't respond. There's no telling what made her freak out like that, but she'll come around eventually. He takes his phone out of his pocket to check for a reply one more time. Still nothing. With his phone already out, he can't resist opening his texts and rereading the last few that he and Whitney have sent to each other. They've been texting a little after they reconnected at the coffee shop the other morning, and she's been on his mind ever since.

"Sir, are you ready to checkout?"

He snaps to attention. "Oh, sorry. Yeah." He pushes his cart forward, letting the salesman scan his purchases. He has got to stop zoning out, he tells himself.

***

"Oh, good grief," Jackson mutters, bending down to clean up the mess from the bag of mulch that ripped open, spilling all over the customer's front walkway. All morning long, Jackson has been so preoccupied with Ellie's strange behavior and thoughts of Whitney that he hasn't been able to fully focus.

His client Mr. Walker is an older man in his seventies. He moved into the neighborhood not long after his wife died. He needed a new start, he'd said. No longer able to do the job himself, he hired Jackson, but he doesn't have anything else to do all day but to hover while Jackson works. Most of the time he can tune the old man out, but it's unnerving always having someone watching your every move.

"Sloppy, kid. Better straighten up." Mr. Walker calls from the front porch.

"Sorry, Mr. Walker." Jackson throws his hand up in acknowledgment and continues cleaning up his mess.

"Got somethin' on your mind?" Mr. Walker laughs, but it quickly turns into a deep, hacking, smoker's cough.

"No sir, it just got away from me is all." He dumps the bulging, ripped bag over by his truck, shaking his head.

The stone pavers clink together as he stacks them up in Mr. Walker's garage. Now that the liner is in place and the mulch is all spread, he's ready to edge the area with them. But it'll have to wait until tomorrow; it's well after six, and Jackson has no plans to stay any longer.

His faithful old truck rumbles to life, but he doesn't move just yet. One more glance at his cell phone shows that Ellie still hasn't returned his texts. It's like they are in two different worlds now, hard to imagine that they were once the closest of all. It's time they had a talk.

16

Dance music blares from her iPhone on the desk. With a deep, calming breath, Ellie tries to center herself as she opens her laptop and refreshes her email once more. Still nothing. She clicks the other open tab, pulling up the awful resume on her locked LinkedIn account. She's emailed customer service about completely disabling the account but still no word. Since her access is barred, there's no way to know how many potential employers have seen this. She wonders if her old boss has. *Oh, God. Has Connor?* The mere thought makes her shudder with a dangerous mix of rage and complete humiliation. So much for centering. Her eyes narrow into dark slits when she thinks of Connor and what he must be up to now. He got what he wanted after all.

She should never have gotten involved with him; aside from them being coworkers, there were several red flags when they met. She just ignored them. It seems to be a habit for her to run to the wrong men. For as long as she lives, she will never forget the 45th anniversary company party just a couple months ago. Not only did she find out she would be promoted to senior designer, but also that her new boyfriend Connor was actually already in a long-term relationship and had brought his actual girlfriend to the party. *Connor.* She says the name out loud, spitting out the syllables in disgust. It wasn't just the fact that he was seeing another woman; it was also how insanely jealous he got when he found out that she would be promoted to senior over him. It wasn't lost on her, the sexist way that he inquired about her qualifications instead of congratulating her even though she had been there longer, and her work reviews were excellent. She worked harder than most, and she knew that she earned that position.

Ellie had waited so long for that night. This was a huge promotion, and she had been waiting her entire life to be recognized for something other than her big doe eyes, glowing skin, or her long mass of perfect hair. She was more than what she looked like, and she was on a mission to prove it. That night was going to be magic; she could be everything; she could be beautiful, smart, successful, and loved. At least that's what she thought. Dressed in a brand-new glittery mist-blue dress and sky-high silver heels, she had twirled around and around, taking in the luxury of the rented banquet hall with its crystal chandeliers and endless buffets of food. It was all set to be the best night of her life, but in walked Connor with his insanely tall and gorgeous girlfriend. There weren't many women who could make Ellie feel insecure, not in the way that Connor's girlfriend had. He was quite the actor that night. As the promotion was announced, he made a scene of being overly affectionate with his date, trying his hardest to make Ellie jealous, spitefully taking away from her moment. He must've learned about her promotion ahead of the event. Why else would he suddenly avoid her and put on such a show with his girlfriend?

Once everyone had gone home and the party was over, Connor wasted no time in trying to sabotage her work. Her sketches went missing. Her computer went out of commission with a mysterious virus; even her assistant; Jean—who Connor was also probably sleeping with—began telling her the wrong times for meetings. The days became miserable. How frustrated she was to appear ditzy and in over her head when she knew she could handle the job. There were whispers about why she had been promoted; she was making her boss look bad. Rumors ran wild. Of course, there was no proof that it was Connor, but she knew. She didn't understand why he couldn't just be happy for her. Why he needed to ruin things for her so badly. And how he could flip from being so sweet to so utterly cold and unfeeling.

The day came when she was called into the head office. Feeling so beaten down, she didn't bother to fight for her reputation or her job. She had lost to a well-liked man with a grudge, and there was no repairing her image. But when her boss insinuated that Connor would be better equipped for the position, the heartbreak and the betrayal became too much for her and something inside of her broke.

She called him. And called him. She didn't stop calling him for 5 days. Leaving tearful messages on his machine, she cycled through begging and accusing, frightening both him and his girlfriend. She waited by his desk at work, not knowing that he had used his vacation days to avoid her after the phone calls began. She just needed closure, she had told herself. Needed to know why. How could someone who was so charming in the beginning do these awful things to her? And, how could he not have told her he was seeing someone else; it was all too much. He ruined their relationship and her job. So, she showed up to his house, and that's when she really snapped. Actually, it was more like a blind-rage blackout. The whole thing ended pretty badly, resulting in a damaged Audi and a restraining order. And the loss of her job. The memory feels like an attack. Resentment rushes through her, and her heart pounds angrily; she paid for what she did, but Connor didn't. Some people never have to pay for their wrongs.

The doorbell chime echoes through the house, breaking through her painful reflections. Grateful to focus on anything other than her time in Minneapolis, Ellie looks out of the guest room window. Outside in the driveway, Jackson's truck sits parked beside her car. *What is he doing here?* Suddenly, her throat feels dry, her hands shake. She isn't ready to talk to him yet—everyone should be together to confront him about the house offer. Maybe, she should have just texted him back, she thinks.

She knew it was coming, but the knock at the bedroom door makes her stomach drop. Jackson walks in before she even has time to answer.

"Jackson, what are you doing here?" Instinctively,

she backs up, nearly tripping over her own feet. *Does he know?*

"Hey, El. Your mom let me in, told me to come on up. When you weren't at the motel, I figured you'd be here. Your parents look great by the way. It's been a while since I've seen them. They haven't changed at all."

"Oh. Yeah," she mumbles. Fixated, she stares at him. Searching the gold and mocha flecks in his eyes for any indications that something isn't right. His eyes betray nothing, and it's frustrating. There once was a time when she could tell what he was thinking simply by the look on his face.

"Ellie." He waves his hand in front of her, breaking her trance. "What's going on with you? You aren't answering my calls or returning my texts. Not to mention the way you ran out of my house like someone was chasing you. El, are you in some kind of trouble?"

"I don't know, am I?" Her voice barely registers a whisper.

"What?"

"No, nothing. It's nothing." She shakes her head. "You should go though; I was kind of in the middle of something. I appreciate the visit but--"

"Are you serious?"

"Yeah, I was just doing some work."

With a tilt of his head, he raises his brows. "I thought you were on vacation."

"Oh, it's just a couple things for the office. You know, can't stay away too long." She forces a laugh, but it comes out high-pitched and all wrong.

He looks past her, focusing on the laptop resting on top of the sleek, lacquered dresser. He moves toward it. A profile picture of Ellie in her powder-blue blazer stares back at him. He sees the LinkedIn logo and looks down to her resume below. The confused and hurt look on his face is obvious, and she silently prays that he won't notice the reason for termination listed. A stormy look passes over his face before he quickly conceals it, and with a sinking feeling in her gut, she knows that he has. Maybe he already knew.

"What's this?" He whirls around on his heel. "You need to tell me what's going on, El. This isn't like you. I hate that we can't talk anymore. If something is wrong—"

"There's not—. It's nothing." Ellie crosses the room in a few steps and slams the laptop shut. "I'm just putting out feelers, looking into my options is all." The look on his face washes her in fear but her anger is growing. He has things he needs to answer for as well. "Who are you to say what's 'like me?' You don't even know me anymore. Anyway, you should probably get going. Like I said, I have some things I need to get done." She wants to tell him that she tried telling him what was wrong. Not just back then but yesterday too. They all did and he didn't believe them, so she keeps her mouth shut. Faking bravado, she crosses her arms and matches his stare.

For a moment, the two just stand there, staring and wondering what secrets are hiding there, just under the surface.

"Ellie, I—" He starts.

"It's okay, Jackson. I just need you to go." She breaks the standoff, moving around him to open the door.

"I just—we need to talk, okay? We need to talk about this soon."

"We will. I promise. But right now, I really am busy." Her fingers tremble slightly as she holds the door open for him.

Full of intensity, he stares at her again, for just a few seconds, but long enough to make her uncomfortable before turning to leave. There are more questions to be answered, but he can tell he won't get anything else from her right now. She's shut herself down. "Alright then."

The door slams behind him, and Ellie collapses onto the bed, a cold sweat breaking out over her skin. Tears prick the corners of her eyes. It shouldn't be like this; she shouldn't have to question Jackson's honesty. Jackson, of all people. The fact that he is lying so easily to her hurts even worse than losing Whitney's friendship.

In a tangle of sheets and pillows lie her phone—like a lifeline, she scoops it up to text Derek and Whitney. There's a new notification at the top of the screen: a Facebook friend request from James Myer. With his tanned and perfect face, even his profile picture is gorgeous. Accepting the request, she forgets the reason she grabbed her phone to begin with. Her lips part into a mischievous grin. She scrolls through his page thinking that things might just be looking up for her. After all, she now has someone much more exciting to talk to, to make her forget all about the Doris house and the mess that it's made of her life.

17

Afolded pile of women's sweaters topples, falling off the display table. Whitney curses under her breath and bends to pick them up. Distracted, she piled them too high. Her manager Carol appears around the corner, and Whitney hurriedly stacks them back up, not wanting her mistake to be noticed. Carol was more than a little aggravated at her for using a sick day during inventory. But, it's not like she can tell Carol the truth, or the fact that ever since that man pulled the snake from her car, she's had this unsettling feeling of being watched. So, she folds the sweaters and straightens the racks and pretends it's all very normal.

It's early still; the store will be opening in just a few minutes, and all of the pre-Thanksgiving Saturday shoppers will be rushing in, and Whitney can't wait because if the store is open and busy, Carol won't have time to hover. She moves on to the wall of jeans and begins stacking and organizing when she sees Carol coming her way. But then, Carol stops, checks her watch and turns around, heading for the front of the store to unlock the doors. A sigh of relief escapes Whitney's lips.

The pre-recorded store announcements begin, and she settles back into the monotony of her work. The calm doesn't last long because as soon as the doors open, Ellie barrels in, making a beeline straight for her. Whitney looks at Carol, but she isn't focused on her anymore; her head is bent over a clipboard, studying the sales goals for the day.

"Whitney! I've gotta talk to you." Breathless, Ellie hitches her purse higher on her shoulder, eyes wide, imploring Whitney to listen to her.

"What are you doing here? I'm working!" Whitney whispers. "My boss is already pissed at me. If she catches me hanging out, I'll be fired."

"Who, her?" Ellie nods in Carol's direction. "She's not even paying attention. I'll be quick."

"Fine. But just a minute."

Carol walks over to talk to an associate setting up a Thanksgiving display and leans in, showing him something on the clipboard. Seizing the opportunity, Whitney grabs Ellie's arm, directing her to the fitting rooms.

"In here." She nudges Ellie inside and closes the door, pushing the lock to the side before turning to her. "What is it?"

"Jackson came to see me yesterday." Ellie whispers.

"Okay, so did you ask him about the offer?" Whitney's hand goes to her hip, annoyance seeping through her gestures. There's no way Jackson could have been behind the horrible things that have happened to her. She saw the concern in his eyes when she told him about the snake. Besides, it may have been years since she's talked to him, but those old confused feelings have surfaced again, and she just can't imagine him ever wanting to do her harm. He's been texting to check in on her daily since they've reconnected. It's hard to understand why he would have those papers in the house, but she just knows there's got to be a good explanation for it.

"No way! Not without you guys. I mean, he was seriously acting strange. Like, he showed up at my parents' house. How did he even know that I left the motel to stay with them?"

"You're staying at your parents' place? Does that mean you're in town for a while longer?"

"That's not what matters here, Whit! His eyes were dodgy; he was stomping around the room, going on and on about us needing to talk. Maybe he guessed why I ran out of his house. Oh God, do you think he knows what I saw?" Ellie's voice raises, teetering on hysterics. She shudders involuntarily.

"No, no way." Whitney whispers, desperately trying to get Ellie to settle down. The last thing she needs is for Carol to burst in here. "He was probably just worried about you, El."

"I don't think so. You didn't see his face. He must have figured out that I know about him trying to buy that house. I mean I was terrified. It felt like a threat."

"Alright, so then let's talk to him. All of us." Whitney reaches to grab her old friend's hand but there is such a disconnect lingering between them still that her hand dangles mid-air for a moment before she draws it back to her side.

"Honestly, I don't think I can."

"This is crazy, El. He used to be one of your best friends. People don't just change that drastically. I'll talk to him myself."

Tugging at her hair nervously, Ellie leans close. "Please be careful, Whit."

"I will, I promise. But for now, if I want to keep my job, I've got to get back to work. I'll talk to you later." Whitney leaves the dressing room, eyes peeled for her manager, and not seeing her, she rushes back over to the jean wall as if she never left.

Dumfounded; Ellie stares at her reflection in the cracked and cloudy mirror. *"If I want to keep my job."* Words spoken so flippantly by Whitney. Ellie knows that she didn't say it on purpose, but that doesn't change the fact that it cut deep. Disgust is written all over Ellie's perfect face, whether it's for her friends or herself, she can't be sure. She leaves the store without saying goodbye, now more than ever convinced that she needs to find a new job and get away from here, fast.
***

"Goodnight, Carol." Whitney says as her boss locks the door behind her and turns to head back to her office. Whitney didn't want to stay late, but she did want to get back in Carol's good graces, so when she was asked if she wanted to work after closing to start prepping for the upcoming Black

Friday sale, she agreed.

The temperature has dropped significantly, and she pulls her coat tighter, but the night's chill creeps down her collar anyway. In the past, she's always felt safe at her job, but now, with the doors locked and only a few cars in the parking lot, she quickens her steps, noticing just how eerie it can be in the dark. The parking lot lamps are few and far between, and the one nearest to her flickers and hums making shadows dance and disappear. A car door closes, and on high alert, Whitney whirls around to look. There aren't many cars around, and there isn't any movement from them. She can't be sure how far away the sound was. Her Camry is in sight, just twenty feet ahead. With a deep breath, Whitney tries to slow her heart rate and continue on toward her car. But the click of footsteps from behind sends her racing to the car in a full-blown panic, not bothering to turn and see who's following her. She throws herself into her car, mashing the lock button and tearing out of the parking lot, buckling her seat belt as she drives away. Only when the car is in motion does she dare to look in the rearview mirror. A tall figure, standing alone in the middle of the lot, shrouded in darkness and seemingly staring her way causes waves of fear to crash over her, sending her pulse soaring.

Quickly, she taps the buttons on her phone, all the while trying to keep her eyes on the road. A little voice in the back of her mind whispers this is how people crash their cars, but she can't pull over now. The person from the parking lot could be anywhere, and it's too dark outside to take that risk.

"Hi, mom." She takes a deep breath, calming herself down. She doesn't want her mom to hear the fear in her voice. "I know Mel has been with you a lot lately, but I'm still at work. Do you think she could stay over with you one more night? We've got a lot of Thanksgiving prep to do."

Lying was a split-second decision. Calling the police is out of the question; what could they do? Besides, she may not have seen what she thought she saw. It could have just been another late-night employee heading to their own car. Her body has been set to fight-or-flight ever since she received that package. But on the chance that it isn't a coworker, she doesn't want to bring Melody home in case that person decides to pay a visit. In fact, she herself doesn't want to be there for that very reason. If that figure in the parking lot is who she thinks it is, they've already been to her house once.

So, with her eyes on the road and casting her phone aside, she drives until she hits the dusty driveway to Jackson's home. Hopefully, he won't mind her showing up out of the blue without calling, but she has to stay somewhere tonight, and regardless of what Ellie says, she's not afraid of him.

18

"**D**on't be silly. I'm actually really glad you stopped by." Jackson takes his eyes off his task of lighting a fire in the fireplace and turns around, balancing on one knee. He's nervous, but he keeps his gaze steady, not letting on. She looks so beautiful, luminous, in the soft glow of the table lamp and fire. He watches as she lets her hair out of its bun, the soft curls cascading around her like a halo. He wonders why he never said anything after that night. They both ended up single not long after, and they had already forever altered their friendship—they would've been so good together, but it was too weird, and eventually, he felt the opportunity had passed. So, he kept his heart to himself and watched her from afar as she got older, graduated, dated, and as she became pregnant, and then a mother. No matter the circumstances, she went through every stage of her life so gracefully, in his eyes.

"Thanks, Jackson. But, um, this is more than just a quick stop-by. I know it's totally an imposition, and it's alright if you say no. Maybe it's weird, but I wondered if I could stay the night? Here, on the couch? She shifts from one foot to the other, feeling incredibly awkward at having to ask, but she doesn't want to answer any questions from her mother, and she no longer feels close enough to Ellie or Derek to ask. They've both grown suspicious of Jackson; she wonders what they might say if they find out. It's not lost on her that this isn't the first time she's wondered about their reactions to her and Jackson. She has to admit that deep down, there's a part of her that likes the thrill of them not knowing. The truth is, she just feels drawn here, to him.

The fire no longer important, Jackson stands, dusting his hands off on his jeans. "Of course, you can. Anything you need, Whit. But I have to ask, why? Is there something wrong at your place? Where's Melody?"

"She's safe."

"Safe? Safe from what?" His head tilts in confusion.

She waffles for a moment, wondering how much to say. It's been obvious that he is a bit skeptical about the whole house thing, but in the end, she decides to just tell him. When his mouth draws into a thin line, she can tell he is thinking of excuses to explain away the mysterious parking lot incident. In order to make him see how serious this is, she knows what she has to do. She takes a deep breath and sits down on his soft couch, gathering her thoughts for just a moment before uncomfortably explaining the gift and figurines that were left on her car.

Sinking down into the armchair by the fireplace, he shakes his head. "Oh, Whitney. Why didn't you tell me any of this before? Are you sure it was a replica of the house? Maybe it wasn't even for you; maybe it was only a dollhouse meant for Mel."

"I'm positive. Everything was the same, down to the gross brown wallpaper on the walls in the room we..."

"Were in." He finishes her sentence, noticing the pink tinge deepening on her cheeks.

"Yeah." Her voice shakes for a moment. "The figurines of us were glued together." She stares into the growing fire, unable to look at his face. "It was put there for me to find; I just don't understand why. Anyway, that's why I'd rather not go home. I don't want to be alone. I couldn't tell who it was in the parking lot, but I swear someone was watching me." Tears silently slide down her face as the shock of the evening wears off, and she realizes this isn't going to stop.

"Aw, Whit," he whispers, "I'm so sorry you're upset. I really, honestly think it's just a joke. Probably Derek or Ellie.

You know how they can be."

Whitney's head snaps up. "A joke? You seriously still think this is a joke? Derek and Ellie are being stalked too and you think it's one of them? Didn't you listen to some of the things that have happened to them? I can't even imagine the things they aren't talking about!"

"Yes, but they could be making it up, you know that." Jackson holds his hands out, pleading with his eyes for her to keep an open mind. He doesn't want the night to end in an argument.

"I saw the burned shed. Would Derek really set fire to his own shed?" Angry, Whitney blows the hair from her face.

"Maybe he would," Jackson says softly.

"And Ellie with the spiders in her bed?" She raises her eyebrows, challenging him.

"Did any of us see them? Could she not have made the whole thing up? This entire mess started when she got back in town, right?"

"It started when the house sold; it's just by chance that that's when she got back." Whitney tries to calm down, and as much as she doesn't trust Ellie or Derek, she can't help but defend them the same way she defended Jackson in front of them. No matter the years, she knows them. They have no reason to do the things that have been done. Every one of them knows that if it was a prank, it's not a funny one. She was sure that by explaining the figurines she could make Jackson understand, but it's useless.

"But what if it's not by chance?" He leans back in his seat, disbelief written all over his face. "I'm not being unreasonable here. Spiders and snakes wind up in weird places sometimes, the dollhouse being similar could be an honest coincidence, and as for the shed, it's been windy the past few nights. It's possible an ember from a nearby fire pit blew that way. Kids could have done that. Just because these things may have happened doesn't mean they have to be connected."

"Okay, so what about you then? Why has nothing happened to you? And, how do you feel about the house selling?"

"What about me? I don't know why I haven't gotten any threatening gifts or animals left for me to find. I don't know! Maybe I didn't anger some imaginary ghost. Or maybe, ya'll are looking so hard for clues that you're finding them anywhere." Annoyed, Jackson raises his voice.

"How do you feel about the house selling?" Whitney quietly asks again.

"I don't feel anything about the house being sold, and I'm not sure why it matters."

Not knowing what else to do, Whitney stands. She's never going to get through to him, and there's no point in arguing anymore. It isn't getting them anywhere, and now she's more frustrated than scared. She could tell him she knows about the offer but she hasn't seen it for herself and if she goes down that path she may fracture their friendship for good. "You're right. I'm sorry to have bothered you." She snatches her purse from the coffee table and turns to the door. "But if you think that I would ever make this kind of thing up, then we're obviously not the same people that we used to be."

"Now, hang on. Wait!" He stands, debating on whether or not to go to her. "I don't know what I believe, but I know that you're upset, and you're obviously afraid of something. I'm sorry. This shouldn't have turned into an argument. You came here wanting to stay, so stay. You can have my room, and I'll take the couch." Arms out and eyes pleading. Now that she's here, he can't let her go.

'I don't know…" Unsure, she glances back at the door.

"I'm sorry. I don't understand what's going on with the three of you, but you know I would never let anything happen to you." The fire crackles and jumps, casting shadows across his face and for the briefest moment, orange flames reflect in his eyes. "I mean it."

Stunned, Whitney's purse slips from her shoulder, but she makes no move to fix it. She's aware that her judgment may be clouded by her past feelings for Jackson, but does that make him a threat? Is there some unhinged animosity that he expertly tucks away inside himself? There certainly seems to be a threat out there, outside of the safety of his home. The situation could turn bad either way. She lets her purse fall to the floor, and the doubt she carries falls with it. "I'll stay, and we won't talk about this anymore tonight. I'd like to go to bed."

"Okay, good. Let me just-I'll be right back." Jackson hurries down the hall leaving Whitney standing alone in the living room. She hears him rummaging around in the bedroom.

The fire looks so inviting on this cold night, and like a moth, she can't help but be drawn to it. Standing in front of the warm flames, Whitney finally takes stock of the sprawling living room. It barely registered in her mind the last time she was here. The furniture is sparse, but cozy. The main feature being the plump leather couch; the light brown, whiskey color is the perfect complement to the antique white walls. A matching ottoman rests in front of it. Besides a corner lamp, the only other furniture is a small wooden table by the door with a bowl for keys and pocket change and the royal blue high-back arm chair that sits empty by the fireplace now that Jackson has left. The walls are mostly bare except for a few landscape canvases, a family portrait, and a large t.v. mounted high up in a corner. His taste is simple, yet classic and inviting.

"Here, take these." He rushes back into the room, almost as if he were afraid she would run while he was away. He pushes an old pair of sweats and a tee shirt into her arms; a confused look streaks across her face as he lays a single toothbrush on top. "It's from a new pack."

"Oh, thanks." She shifts the weight of the pile in her arms and looks at him expectantly. "I'm pretty tired so…"

"Oh! Right. Let me show you my room." Leading her down the long hallway, he makes no effort to open any doors or give the full tour of his home. They reach the last room on the left, and he lingers back, letting her enter first.

The room smells like varnish and oakmoss and she feels like a stranger invading an intimate space.

"Well, here we are," he says, chiding himself for

stating the obvious. "I'm sorry there is no television, I'm not really a t.v. in the bedroom kind of person. But the bathroom is right over there." He points to the room beside the closet. "If you get hungry, there's food in the kitchen. I'll just be out in the living room."

Whitney nods her thanks, not knowing what to say. Here she is standing in Jackson's bedroom with him, and the awkwardness is almost too much. The bedside lamp covers the room in a romantic glow and plays against the amber flecks in his eyes. His dark wavy hair, a sharp contrast to the military style he used to wear, but she likes it. Sure that he can sense the confusion swirling in her mind– whether she can trust him, how she feels about him– she turns away, staring at the low-slung moon shining through the open curtains.

"Alright. I'll let you get settled. Goodnight, Whitney." His mouth opens as if he wants to say more, but he closes it, looking down at his socked feet.

"Goodnight." She drops the pile in her arms onto the bed. "Oh, and Jackson?"

He pauses by the door, turning back to face her.

"Thanks for this."

"Of course. See you in the morning." Smiling at her, he leaves and quietly shuts the door behind him.

The bright yellow moon calls to her, and she wanders over to the window, looking out across the woods. Her eyes search the hickory trees in the darkness, and she wonders if the danger is out there among them. A yawn overtakes her, and she realizes how tired she is, now that the adrenaline has worn off. She grabs the sweats and toothbrush from the bed and takes them into the bathroom with her. The tile shower looks so inviting, and she would love to relax under the hot water, washing the day away but even in the bathroom with the bedroom door closed, she feels too vulnerable. Too exposed. So, she ties her hair back, brushes her teeth, and washes her face with the soap on the counter.

His sweats are several sizes too big for Whitney, but they are comfortable, and they smell just like the bedroom— clean and earthy. With another yawn, she climbs into his bed, ready to fade into the oblivion of sleep. But something he said earlier keeps tugging at her, worrying her. She remembers the look on his face as he told her that he didn't know what was going on with the three of them, but he would never let anything happen to her. *Her.* He didn't say anything about keeping Ellie or Derek safe. Turning over on the pillow to face the door, she wonders if he meant anything by it. Surely, he cares what happens to the others. He was just trying to reassure her; he probably just misspoke, she tells herself. Still; it takes her a long time to stop replaying their conversation in her head, quit picking every word apart, and go to sleep.

She wakes before the sun, anxious to get back to Melody. In a move reminiscent of her college days, she gathers last night's outfit from the floor and puts it back on, ready for a hot shower and fresh clothes. In the light of the morning, things never seem as bad, and so Whitney wonders if she overreacted last night. It's obvious someone is messing with them, but maybe her nerves were too frazzled, too tightly wound, and the mystery stalker from the parking lot really was just another employee heading toward their car. They were probably staring at her because she took off running like a maniac. Heat spreads through her cheeks. She feels slightly ridiculous for turning up on Jackson's doorstep late at night and arguing with him. His reaction wasn't what she expected, and as much as she didn't want it to, it concerned her, made her just a little suspicious of him. He claimed that the house selling had no effect on him, not once mentioning the fact that he tried to buy it. If it really is all that innocent, then why would he hide that? *God, now I sound like Ellie.*

Quickly, she makes the bed, folding the borrowed sleepwear and stacking it neatly on top. She needs to be at home with her daughter and away from all of this. So, she scoops up her purse and quietly moves down the hallway, only briefly pausing to look at Jackson asleep on the couch. His long, dark eyelashes flutter on the tops of his cheeks, and he sleeps deeply and unbothered. Her conflicted feelings burn in the pit of her stomach, and without a sound, she walks out the front door, more confused than before.

19

Derek slams the door to his house and races down the porch to his car, the brisk morning wind barely registering. He hasn't been able to stop thinking about the girls' visit a few nights ago. Something just doesn't feel right, but he can't figure out exactly what. The idea that Jackson is the one to leave the matches in his mailbox and set fire to his shed is devastating, but maybe not quite as ridiculous as he had thought. The guy can be tough to read. He needs to know for sure. It just doesn't gel with the Jackson that he grew up with, but they've all had their practice of burying parts of themselves deep down.

One thing is certain; he can't sit around trying to figure it out, so Derek drives. The sun is just barely starting to peak over the horizon. He chases it, flying down the roads until he reaches the house. The Doris house.

The car idles as he sits, watching, hoping to not wake the nosy neighbors that he has come to fear just as much as the house itself. The place is creepy, cloaked in early morning shadows. He remembers the spiders and the snake and all of the things he and the girls have shared with each other, and all of the things he's kept to himself. Staring at the house, he hopes for his mind to clear, for it to make sense. What is it that he isn't seeing? But, all there is are the large barren trees, the dirty white paint chipping off the frame of the place, a few weak and broken porch steps, and the SOLD sign lingering in the yard amongst the dead leaves. He snaps a picture with his phone; perhaps looking it over later might shake something loose. Frustrated, he smacks the steering wheel and hangs his head in defeat. A house can't haunt you if you aren't inside of it, but people can.

The hum of a garage door snaps him to attention. Brake lights from the neighbor's car shine as the door continues to raise. Not wanting to be spotted, Derek throws the Mustang into gear and tears off down the road, not stopping until he reaches an intersection, cursing himself for even going there in the first place. He was just so sure that looking at it up closely might allow some missing pieces to fall into place.

Now realizing it wasn't fully thought-out, the plan was to have some sort of epiphany at Doris's, then go talk to the girls, but there's nothing to tell. He could go home, but Derek quickly dismisses that idea. He can't stand the thought of pacing through the house or sitting nervously on the couch without knowing anything. And even though it's Sunday, he turns the car around and heads into Charlotte to go to the office. Since he comes and goes mostly on his own schedule, he has a key, and there is plenty of work to do on the accounts he's handling. Anything to distract himself.

The car has barely been shut off before he leaps out, slamming the door behind him. So focused on getting into the building and throwing himself into work, he doesn't notice the silver Lincoln that's also parked in front of the office.

His chair groans as he rolls it forward and turns on his computer. He unlocks the desk cabinet and reaches in but remembers the three manila folders stacked neatly on the desk in his bedroom at home. Even though he didn't plan on coming in today, it bothers him to be unprepared. A true type A personality; he loves things to be perfectly organized and planned out. Sighing and drumming his fingers on the desk, he stares for a moment at the login screen. There are still a couple of things he can do without the folders. Typing in his password, he waits for the screen to load. He clicks the accounts icon and begins to type in another access code.

A throat clears behind Derek, and he jumps, knocking a cup of pens over. They scatter and roll one by one off of the desk as he slowly turns around, heart banging in his chest.

"Oh! Mr. Clarke, I didn't know you were here." He coughs, hand to chest and wishing for his racing heart to settle.

"I would imagine not." Mr. Clarke, the owner of the agency, is a workaholic well past retirement age, but never one to take a break or, apparently, a day off. He stands at an intimidating 6'4 height and has a head full of thick white hair. Normally, his imposing image is softened by the wrinkles that crease around his eyes as he smiles. There are no creasing wrinkles, nor any smiles on his face today. "Derek," he pauses, sighing and rubbing a hand across his forehead. "Derek, I was going to wait until tomorrow to talk to you about something, but since you're here now, I might as well go ahead and do it. Why are you here today, by the way?"

"I um, just wanted to get a few things done. Get on top of a couple of my renewed accounts." He stares up at Mr. Clarke, but finds it hard to meet his gaze. He doesn't return the question. It's well known throughout the office that after Mr. Clarke's wife passed and his kids moved away that he comes in, finding something to busy himself every day of the week. Derek's boss has a reputation for being slightly tough and a hard worker who pushes his people to be their best, but right now the look in his eye is downright frightening.

"Uh huh. And would those accounts happen to be the Spencers, the Ambers, and Mr. Collins?" He tilts his head, trying to read Derek's expression.

"Yeah, why? They've been with us forever; they haven't suddenly changed their minds about renewal, have they?"

"That would be putting it mildly, Derek. Why don't we talk in my office for a moment?" All the desks around are empty with most people off enjoying their weekend, but it's a power move. Talks like this need to be had in the boss's office. Mr. Clarke is nothing if not a traditional sort of leader.

Derek looks to his boss dumbfounded; he realizes he may have been a little distracted over the past week but nothing to warrant the cancellation of contracts. He has handled these clients since he first started working here. They wouldn't suddenly all complain about him. Would they? He slowly gets up and follows Mr. Clarke to his office at the front of the building, head hung low as if headed for execution.

"Go ahead, have a seat." Mr. Clarke waves his hand to the two chairs in front of his large desk as he settles into his oversized leather chair.

"I'm sorry Mr. Clarke, but you're going to have to fill me in on what's happened because I'm at a loss."

"Derek, I understand that you've been working with these clients for a while now, so I'll try to be as delicate about this as possible." Visibly uncomfortable with what he has to say, Mr. Clarke shifts in his seat.

Derek leans forward, anxious to find out why three happy clients could suddenly decide to up and leave.

"Friday I received some upsetting phone calls. Mr. Spencer, Mrs. Amber, and Mr. Collins, all calling to inform me that they've had their identity stolen."

"Oh, that's awful. But—"

"Yes, well they each discovered fraudulent activity exactly two days after signing their renewal papers. With you. You see where I'm going, son?" He hooks his hands together, resting his chin on top.

"Mr. Clarke, surely you don't think that I had anything to do with this, I would never steal anyone's identity, or anything for that matter!" Throwing his hands up, he begs for Mr. Clarke to see the truth. But all the steam is gone when he realizes who would do something like this, someone who has been doing a lot of things like this lately. Someone connected to that damn house. If that's the case, then they've probably made sure to make him look as guilty as possible. There will likely be a million ways that this points back to him.

"Tell me then; why has the password to access your files changed? I got I.T. to get past it but once we did, the last three accounts opened were, well you can guess." Mr. Clarke looks at him hard, his expression slowly transitioning from anger to something of pity. "You've always been a great worker, one of my best. Why in the world would you do a thing like this? Help me to understand; are you having financial problems?"

"Financial problems? What? No! Mr. Clarke, I didn't change the password. I don't know who did, but I didn't do this. I didn't even know it had been changed. I hadn't even logged into my accounts yet. Those three accounts were the last accessed because I have been inputting their paperwork this week. That's all."

"I wish I could believe you, son. But I've got to keep this agency scandal free. I've managed to find a way to do that, and for you to avoid criminal charges. Your paycheck along with money that I'll be fronting, will be used to pay back what was stolen. And there's no getting around it; the clients agreed to this with the condition that you would be let go."

Not trusting his own voice, Derek whispers, "Are you serious?"

"I'm afraid so."

"I didn't do this, Mr. Clarke. Someone must've set me up, but I didn't. Like I said, I wouldn't."

Mr. Clarke mashes his lips together in something of a sympathetic smile; he's always felt a sort of fatherly protectiveness for Derek. But if he is a thief, then he has to go. "I'm sorry, kid."

Humiliated and with nothing left to say, Derek is grateful at least that he isn't behind bars. He slumps out of the office, defeated, and quickly gathers his things from his desk before leaving. With watery eyes, he throws his belongings in the back of the mustang, crashes into the seat and stomps the accelerator, flying down the road with little regard for the speed limit. Things like that don't seem to matter as much right now. Ellie and Whitney will believe him; they've endured too much lately not to, but Derek is going to make sure that Jackson believes them this time. Finally, he has a purpose, a mission to throw himself into, and he won't stop until Jackson understands.

20

It's cold and quiet in the house; the fire from last night has long fizzled out. Jackson startles awake, confused and twisted up like a pretzel from a night on the couch. Sitting up and stretching the knots from his back, it comes back to him--the reason for his uncomfortable sleeping situation. *Whitney was here last night. Whitney!* She came to him, needed him, he remembers. The thought of her sleeping over draws him from the couch toward his bedroom. He won't wake her up, just check to see if she's still asleep. Thinking he can make her a nice, warm breakfast where they can sit and talk over grits and bacon, he smiles to himself as he raises a fist to knock on the door. Only, the door isn't shut; it's wide open and the light is off. The bed is made and not a single possession of hers is on the floor or dresser. He blinks slowly a few times as if that could suddenly make her appear. But it can't; she's gone.

Weak sunlight splashes through the window, the soft blue curtains not completely drawn. A cheerful sight mocking the sinking feeling in his stomach. The door to the bathroom stands ajar. The lights are off, but he checks the room anyway. He can't help but be disappointed; remembering that she was here had been a welcome comfort, an early morning jolt--however brief. She could have gone anywhere else, but she came here, to him. Her gardenia perfume still lingers softly in the air.

He slinks back out of the room, resigned to eating his

breakfast alone. His phone glows from where it lay on the arm of the couch. Eagerly he grabs it on his way to the kitchen. It's just a text from J.J.---one of his regular teens looking for some holiday work. Disappointed, he hurls it at the couch, unreasonably upset that the text wasn't from Whitney. Yesterday morning, the text would have made no difference to him, but Whitney showing up changed all that; it changed everything.

Bacon crackles and sizzles in the pan and unlike most mornings, the alluring scent of it does nothing for Jackson. He goes through the motions, cooking his meal more out of habit than want. Whitney only stayed one night, but her absence can be felt throughout the space. The house suddenly seems empty in a way that it never has before. With his mind on her, he doesn't notice the grease begin to bubble. A large pop interrupts the quiet of his thoughts, a smattering of boiling grease slapping him in the face. The pain doesn't register, but the fact that he eats alone does. The last dregs of his tasteless breakfast are washed down with a sip of coffee. Twirling his mug around with his fingers, he tries to figure out why Whitney would leave without saying goodbye. She didn't mention having to work today. She may have still been angry with him after their argument, or maybe she just needed to go get Melody. But couldn't she have had breakfast first, at least said something to him before leaving? After years of not speaking, they suddenly seem to be thrust into this thing; what, he isn't yet sure. He does know it revolves around that old house, but the reason is a total mystery to him. He wonders if it's too late to tell Whitney about the offer he made on the place. Maybe he doesn't have to. It's not like he ended up buying it, and anyway, it wasn't his best idea. He groans; he never should have been so dismissive of her fear; after all, an exact replica of the house showing up out of the blue is probably not random. He can almost feel that old wallpaper crinkling behind his back. Even though he doesn't believe it all, he decides to involve himself more for the sake of Whit.

With a swift motion, he slams the mug down onto the table. Not one to mope, he refuses to sit around wondering. Sundays are the only days he takes for himself, and his yard desperately needs work. He's so busy with his client's yards that his is often left neglected. All of these games someone is playing are for children, and he doesn't have time for that. He throws on a fresh pair of jeans and an old t-shirt and laces up his boots.

The morning is cool, and the sunlight has been replaced with soft gray clouds, but the fresh air calms him. From his spot on the porch, he looks around the vast lawn at all the fallen leaves that need to be cleared. A lot of problems can be thought through by the repetition of monotonous grunt work. The perfect way to figure out how to mend things with Whitney. Quickly, he descends the three steps of the porch, not noticing the large pile of leaves directly underfoot. The mass of brown and golden yellow foliage doesn't make that satisfying crunch as he steps down, instead, they give way.

Leaves flutter up and slowly float back down as Jackson loses footing and falls mid-step into a four-foot hole. The cry that forces its way from his mouth scares the birds from the nest they've made in his browning fern. The awkward step crunches his body, one leg landing hard at the bottom while the other twists up slamming into his chin as his hips painfully meet the earth. Only head and shoulders peeking out above the hole while below his body lay trapped, contorted into positions not natural for a person to be in. Blinking wildly, he looks around, his head the only thing he can manage to move, and he struggles to understand what's happened. He walks this spot directly in front of his porch every day, and this hole wasn't here yesterday. But, the pain in his left leg is too strong to focus his mind on anything other than the agony spreading throughout his body. His breath catches, his ribs on fire, and with his thoughts coming too quickly, too jumbled; he looks upward to the swirling clouds before everything goes black.

21

Determined, Derek sails down the dirt road, trees flying past making him dizzy and nauseated, but it only adds to his motivation. Not bothering to watch the path, he bumps over several small branches blown across the drive and doesn't notice Jackson's limp figure until he is right up next to him.

"Oh, my God!" He finally makes out Jackson's broken body with his head slumped and unmoving at his chest. Derek slams on the brakes to avoid hitting his friend, and the dirt and debris jumble under his tires as he skids, spinning out until finally his bumper connects with a stump, punctuating the air with a loud crunch. His Mustang is everything to him, but the damage to the car never crosses his mind. He pushes the car door open with such force that it flies back, smacking him right in the shoulder. What on any other day would be incredibly painful is now just a mere hindrance to getting to Jackson.

"Jackson!" He screams, knowing that his friend can't hear him. All of his suspicions of Jackson vanish like smoke as he fears the worst. The ground seems intent on tripping him up but he makes it to the hole, falling to his knees. He has no idea what he's supposed to do in this situation, but he screams Jackson's name over and over as he shakes Jackson's listless shoulders. A sob overpowers him while he looks down into the hole at the mangled limbs resting at the bottom. Hoping for a miracle, he slaps Jackson's face a few times to no avail.

Finally, it dawns on him to check for a pulse. Taking great caution, he moves his hand to Jackson's chest. Tears of relief flow freely from his eyes when he feels the rise and fall of the heart beat beneath Jackson's shirt.

Sliding back but still maintaining a protective closeness, Derek reaches in his back pocket for his phone. He dials 911 first before calling Ellie and Whitney. After reassurance that medical help is on the way, and promising to let the girls know when they get to the hospital, he hits the off button for his phone screen and leans back. The fading adrenaline has left him with an awful headache and a throbbing shoulder.

There's nothing to be done but to wait, so he whispers calming words to Jackson, knowing that they won't be heard but hoping they are anyway. The hole looks jagged, not perfectly round, but something about it just doesn't feel right to him. All the leaves scattered about seem uncharacteristic of Jackson. He always takes care to clear them, especially the ones right in front of his walkway. The cold November air seeps right into Derek's bones, and he knows that whatever or whoever is behind all of this has once again taken things up a notch. The ambulance is taking forever. He's left waiting out here, exposed to anyone who could be watching from the crush of the trees. Still, he resolves not to hide in his car; he won't leave Jackson alone.

After several long minutes, the ambulance races down the driveway in a flurry of action, followed closely by the responding officer. All of a sudden, they aren't alone any longer. There are people scattered everywhere barking out commands, telling him to move this way, asking if he is hurt, if he knows what happened.

Circling Jackson, the officer peers down into the hole before straightening up and walking toward the house and back through the yard, scanning over everything as he makes his way toward the garage, disappearing inside for a moment. The static from his radio cuts through the noise, hurling Derek's mind back in time. He responds to the voice on the other end of the radio and heads back over to the center of the activity.

"Someone did this! It wasn't an accident!" Derek yells, catching the attention of the officer.

The officer, young, somewhere in his late twenties, looks up, taking note of Derek's frenzied raving. He feels for the guy; he can tell they're close in age and he knows that anyone can be driven to hysterics when a loved one is badly injured. He moves toward Derek. He's relatively new to the force but carries himself with a confidence that comes with growing up in a police family.

"Hi, Officer Davidson." He reaches for a handshake, hoping it will have a steadying effect.

"Derek Steven. My friend is hurt, I think someone caused this." He shakes the officer's hand roughly, not bothering to settle down.

"Did you see your friend get pushed?" Officer Davidson's gaze hardens.

"No sir, I got here after he fell." Derek, still frantic, shakes his head.

"Can you tell me why you think this wasn't an accident? Because to me, it looks like your friend just didn't notice a little hole in the yard."

"A little hole?" Derek yells. "That's not a little hole, Officer. It's got to be almost a four-foot drop!"

"Well, maybe so, but I'm not seeing any evidence to the contrary. Let me tell you what I do see." The officer points to the open garage. "There's a couple dirty rakes and shovels leaning up against the house over there. And over that way, a truck with a decal on the side that reads; GRAY LANDSCAPING." Officer Davidson shrugs. "What's your friend's name, sir?"

"Jackson Gray." Derek whispers, resigned.

"Look, I understand this is your friend and you're concerned, but it looks like your buddy's been doing some of his own landscaping and just had a misstep. See all these leaves; they probably just blew around, and he didn't see the hole until it was too late. Might've dug up a stump or was getting ready to plant a tree and just misjudged where the hole was after the leaves fell."

"That'd have to be a giant tree to go in a hole that

deep." Derek scoffs.

Officer Davidson regards Derek with growing interest. He stands tall, hands on his duty belt. "You seem spooked. Someone you know of want to hurt you or your friend?"

"Yeah, maybe. I mean, I'm not sure but…"

"You got any names?" Davidson's eyebrows raise in surprise.

"No—I just…" Derek mashes his lips together, wondering how to explain why someone may want to hurt Jackson. He wants Officer Davidson to see that it wasn't an accident, but there's no way to do that without dragging Ellie and Whitney into it. And then they'd have to come clean about the house, and what they did in there. "No, you're probably right; he must've misjudged his step." Derek says. There's no way that Jackson would ever make a mistake like this, and along with everything else that has been happening, Derek knows deep down it was intentional. He's never going to make the cop see that without real evidence, so he nods his thanks and walks over to the ambulance.

Helplessly, he watches as they look over Jackson, and when they pull his unconscious body from the hole, he has to look away. They load Jackson onto the stretcher and roll him toward the vehicle. The bones in his leg stick out at odd angles.

A woman in uniform turns to Derek with sympathy in her eyes and softly shakes her head. "I'm sorry sir, but you'll have to follow in your own car."

Head hung low, Derek trudges back toward his busted-up Mustang.

22

The skin on her left thumb is ripped and raw from nervous picking. Not only is she scared for Jackson— terrified really— but she's worried about Melody. Whitney hadn't been at her mother's house long at all before she received the call about Jackson's fall, and the disappointment on her daughter's plump little face when she began to explain that she needed to leave again was enough to make her consider not even coming to the hospital today. She thought about waiting until tomorrow, when Mel was back in school, to come see him, but it can't be helped; he needs his friends right now, and they need to figure out what is going on before things get any worse.

Horrified, she drove silently to the hospital, no usual music playing—just the lonely sound of the blinker as she indicated each turn. She cycled through her emotions, one moment feeling helpless and scared that he could be paralyzed or worse, and the next, anxious of what might have happened to her if she had stayed over at his place any longer. Guilt burns deep in her heart for thinking of herself, but still, it's a question that can't be ignored. She was at his house just this morning. What could've happened? Even though the haunting figure in the parking lot last night sent her running to Jackson, she hadn't fully grasped how much danger they're all in—until now. No other information was given other than Jackson fell in a hole and is unconscious; that's what Derek said over the phone. And just as she was hanging up, she heard him whisper; "It wasn't an accident. You know what this was." Her blood runs ice cold as she remembers the strained murmur in Derek's voice, as if he didn't want to be overheard.

So, she sits in silence next to Ellie, shredding her thumb and listening to the non-slip nurses' shoes squeak across the floor. A painting of a sailboat hangs on the wall of the tiny waiting room, catching her attention. Whitney stares at the picture, not bothering to look over at Ellie as she loudly adjusts her body in the thinly cushioned, hard-backed chair. The painting's colors fade and swirl into undecipherable blues and whites as her vision goes in and out of focus. Blinking slowly, she feels an exhaustion that she hasn't felt since Melody was a colicky newborn.

Finally, she breaks her gaze from the painting to sneak a glance at Ellie, who looks just as distressed and worn-out as herself. Her heart clenches when she sees Ellie try to discreetly wipe a tear from under her eye. She must be feeling awful after blaming Jackson for everything they've been dealing with, but even though Whitney herself didn't put much stock in the accusations, she can understand why Ellie felt the way she did.

"El, you didn't know," she whispers.

Her red-rimmed eyes lift to meet Whitney's concerned face. "I basically accused one of my oldest friends of stalking us and all but threw him out of my house."

Whitney puts her hand on top of Ellie's, keeping it there even as Ellie flinches. "You thought it was him; he tried to buy the house. Even I can admit that it's weird. He didn't tell us anything. Nothing had happened to him; you couldn't have known he would get hurt." She squeezes Ellie's hand, offering her a small smile. "Jackson doesn't blame you; you know."

Ellie rips her hand away, holding it protectively down by her side. "How do you know that? Did you ask him if he blames me? Because I'm pretty sure you aren't going to get an answer from an unconscious guy."

"Jackson loves you; he always has. You're the sister he never had, El, and even though it's been a long time, he's never stopped caring. I'm sure of that."

"You would know."

"What?"

"Nothing." Ellie shakes her head, wishing she hadn't made such a rude comment. Whitney has been trying hard lately, and Ellie is done holding onto that grudge. But sometimes, old wounds take a long while to heal. "I just meant; you probably know him better than I do now. I haven't been around."

"Oh."

The conversation is interrupted before it even gets off the ground; Derek rushes in the room red-faced and out of breath. "Guys, he's awake."

"Oh, my God." Whitney breathes.

"He's asking for y'all."

Both women slowly stand, each reckoning with themselves over how they've recently let Jackson down.

"So, how is he?" Ellie's tone matches her pace, slow and careful.

"Pretty good, considering." Derek shrugs. "I mean, someone did carve out a death trap on his property."

"Great choice of words." Whitney's soft voice grows hard.

"Sorry. He's not getting out of here today, but he is much better. The doctor says he has a concussion, a couple fractured ribs, and a broken fibula."

Whitney's emotions go unchecked as she gasps, eliciting stares from her friends. "I'm sorry, guys. It's just that, I guess I was expecting the worst, and even though his injuries aren't life-threatening, it's just, hearing it out loud makes it so real, you know?"

"I know what you mean." Ellie twists her hair back off her shoulders.

"Me too. After seeing him like that. Well, this is a relief." Derek nods, taking Whitney's arm to guide her down the hallway.

Ellie follows close behind, working hard at removing the jealous look from her face. Never has he offered his arm to her. Beautiful, little Ellie, somehow always last in line. "So, what did the cops say?" She asks a little too loudly.

Derek stops, dropping Whitney's arm. "That it was his own fault." A dark storm passes over his eyes. "They think he must've dug the hole himself, being that he does landscaping, and that leaves settled around it. They think he just forgot and stepped right in."

"That's ridiculous. I mean just last—" Whitney clamps her mouth shut before she finishes. She's got to be more careful. They don't need to know that she was over at Jackson's last night. It might not be a big deal any longer if they don't suspect him, but the fact that she left his place unscathed might draw their suspicions to her.

"Last what?" Ellie crosses her arms knowingly. Insecurities flood her thoughts.

"Well, just last time we were over there, there weren't any holes." Whitney turns away, facing the long hallway, aware of how red her face gets when caught in a lie.

"Uh huh. So, what's the plan? We all go to the police and tell them that? Wait for them to speak to Jackson?"

"I already tried telling them he didn't dig any holes. That cop looked at me like I was nuts. He would never believe any of us. He wrote it off; they won't be coming to question him. I'm sure of that. But, I can poke around, try to find something concrete to take to them. I'll make it my sole mission before anyone else gets hurt." He remembers his frustration with the Doris house this morning just before being fired; it feels like it was ages ago. The weight of what is happening settles all around him, and for a moment, he panics. What if he can't figure this thing out? What if whoever is responsible takes it even further? It's impossible to fight an enemy that you can't see.

He imagines himself, standing on the tattered and stained floor in the dark office of that dirty, old house. A match in hand—all it would take was one strike, but then the sirens came. He was ready. He could've done anything he needed to back then. Calling up a newfound purpose from his dark memories, he straightens his shoulders and hardens his jaw. He couldn't keep them together then, but he can now. "After everything this morning, trust me. Come on." He turns and continues, leading them to room 1215.

As the three walk up, they notice that someone else has already beaten them to Jackson's room. A familiar man is standing in front of the door, staring down at his brown dress shoes, and nervously running his hands through his hair.

"James?" Ellie asks, confused.

"Oh, hi guys." James turns, a sheepish look flashes over his face.

"What are you doing here?" Derek's body stiffens.

James runs a hand over his freshly shaved chin. "Oh, one of my buddies was finishing his patrol when he heard the call come in for Jackson's place. We were supposed to meet up, and he let me know, so I thought I would come and pay him a visit, see how he's doing."

"Are the cops even allowed to give out that kind of information?" Whitney whispers to Derek.

"I have no idea," He whispers back. He can't take his eyes off James; the guy standing in front of him looks so different from the kid they knew so long ago. No wonder Ellie was going on about him the way she was. It's a drastic change, definitely in the guy's favor. "But why'd you come though? I didn't know the two of you were even close."

His face ashen, James feels almost transported back to high school, trying to make these guys like him and he just stands there, awkward and not knowing how to respond.

"Geez Derek, I didn't know you had an approved list of visitors." Ellie's voice hardens. "Obviously Jackson has other friends you know. It's not like James is a stranger. Some people care about others."

"It's okay, Ellie." James offers her a smile before turning back to Derek. "Jackson and I ran into each other a while back and keep in touch sometimes. I heard he was hurt, and I just wanted to check on him, make sure he's alright. I'm sorry to impose. I know how close you all are."

"It's just weird is all I'm saying." Derek shrugs. It always bothered him the way James seemed to hang around when they were younger, the way he stared at Ellie and attempted to appeal to Whitney's empathy. The fact that James and Jackson kept in touch irks him. They didn't need another friend back then and they don't now.

"Derek, lay off." Whitney elbows him in the ribs. "I'm going in to see him."

"Fine. I'll be there in a sec." Derek speaks to Whitney but doesn't bother to break his stare with James. After losing his job and finding his best friend unconscious, his pride is hurt and he's out to put that shame onto someone else.

"Ellie, can I speak to you alone for a moment? I'm so glad I ran into you even if it's at the hospital." James runs his hand down her shoulder, letting it rest on her lower back. He moves to lead her a few steps down the hall to a secluded corner but not before turning back to face Derek, giving him a perfect, bright smile sending him into a quiet rage.

23

"It's just one date, ok? Chill out." Ellie fluffs her hair, staring at her reflection in the mirror above the sink in Jackson's hospital room.

"All I'm saying is, don't you think it's strange? He shows up to Jackson's room out of nowhere, asks you out, stays all of three minutes, and then leaves. I don't know, something's off with that guy." His hands sweat, and his chest tightens. It's back—that same out of control feeling Derek used to get when he couldn't influence his friend's choices. He tries to fight the feeling, but his anger swells. So what if it's her life; she has terrible judgment, he thinks.

He can't remember when it started; this need to control everyone's lives around him. As a teenager, he liked the drama, knowing the ins and outs of everybody's private lives—he told himself he was just being helpful, giving a point of view that they couldn't see. But by college, it had blossomed into something ugly, compulsion to move people around like pieces on a chessboard. The power he felt from planting a few seeds and then sitting back to see if things play out the way he wants. He kept it hidden as best as he could but then that night…they were starting to drift, and he had to stop it. His hand itches. He rubs it along the side of his pants; he can almost feel the matchbook against his skin. He should've talked to someone, seen a therapist, but that night made him realize how dangerous his thoughts could be, and when his group of friends actually did fall apart, he did his best to keep only superficial relationships, to take as little interest in other's lives as he could manage. He did better for a while. Now, it feels as if it's all at stake again. Besides, they have their demons too.

Struggling to sit up straighter; Jackson winces. "Let it go Derek. He's a decent enough guy. Ellie's a grown woman; she can date whoever she wants." His eyes slide to Ellie, meeting her gaze in the mirror, a soft smile plays at her lips as she mouths "Thank you."

"Fine, go on your date, but I for one am more concerned with who dug the giant hole in Jackson's yard."

Ellie whips around, lightening on her face. "Are you serious right now? I'm just as concerned about this, about him, I'm here aren't I?"

"Yeah, you're here. Preening in the mirror while Whit and I actually worry about Jackson. God, Ellie. Look at him, fractured ribs, broken leg, a concussion for crying out loud. But go ahead; put on some more lipstick."

Ellie's hands tremble at her sides while her words are dangerously calm. "You should watch what you say."

"That's enough!" Jumping from the chair she's been sitting in, Whitney inserts herself between the two. "That's enough. I'm sick of this. Derek, you need to lay off her, or you can leave, and, Ellie, I really don't care who you date, but maybe tonight isn't the night for dinner and movie, got it?"

"This whole thing is putting everyone on edge. I'm sorry that I didn't believe you guys when you first told me, but obviously I do now." Jackson weakly motions to his leg. "You guys wouldn't be fighting like this if someone wasn't trying to hurt us."

"We wouldn't even be speaking."

"Not helpful, Ellie. Now look; I understand the police assumed it was an accident, but I don't understand why I can't just call them and tell him I haven't dug any holes."

Derek steps toward the bed, suddenly exhausted. He waffles for only a moment. It wouldn't be the worst thing for the police to handle it—they could probably figure it out and end this whole thing, but his pride was hurt. In a way, he's glad Officer Davidson didn't listen because now he sees the opportunities in the situation. He can solve it himself and embarrass the officer and he can be the one to end it and save his friends. He'll have to sell it though. "You have a concussion, Jackson. They'll think you forgot. Maybe they'll think you're embarrassed that you fell and are just trying to save face for the sake of your job. That cop saw your dirty shovels and he was convinced it was an accident."

"That's ridiculous," Ellie starts.

Derek puts up a hand, silencing her. "It's not. Look, I'm sorry for what I said, but Jackson calling the police is not going to get them to do anything. They'll say they'll look into it, but we all know they have more important stuff to take care of. I'm gonna handle this one."

Sure, the cops may take Jackson at his word and check into it, but there's no benefit in them solving it. The four of them are just starting to come back together— Derek knows that if he can find out who's behind it all and stop them by himself, he would be a hero, their hero.

"Handle it how, exactly?" Whitney moves closer to Jackson, taking his hand in hers, not bothering to care who notices.

"Don't worry about that. I'll figure out what's going on, and I'll take care of it. That's all that matters."

"I'm not sure I'm okay with it but; do what you need to do, just be careful. I mean it, man." Jackson squeezes Whitney's hand. He hopes Derek can sense the seriousness in his voice; he didn't believe them before, but after his fall, he doesn't want to see any of them hurt.

"No problem. Anyway, did the doctor tell you how long you'll be here?"

Shifting uncomfortably in the small hospital bed, Jackson sits up, allowing Whitney to fuss over the pillows behind him. "Just a few days. I'll have to come back for them to check out my ribs and leg, but I can continue to heal at home."

"No way." Whitney fluffs the pillows, placing them gently back on the bed. She feels the stares from Derek and Ellie boring into her back, but she pays them no attention.

This whole mess today has brought out feelings for Jackson that she wasn't aware she still had, but this time, she doesn't care if the others see it. "Not happening, you have a broken leg. I'm not letting you hobble around your house. If you trip, you could mess up your ribs even worse. You'll stay at my place."

"But you've got Melody and work."

"So, I'll take the rest of my sick days, and Mel will love having someone around to watch cartoons with her. Besides, Ellie is at her parent's place, and Derek's plans don't really sound safe while you're trying to heal."

"Alright, you win. I'll let you know as soon as they release me. So El, when is this date happening?"

A string dangling from the bottom of her blouse catches Ellie's attention, and she pulls at it before smiling up at Jackson, embarrassed. The guilt from lying to him and pushing him away is written all over her face. She can't believe she ever thought he would hurt her. "Tomorrow night, just going to the movies."

"Well, I hope you have fun." He gives her a small wink. With those few words, all their tension evaporates. Nine years of a dead friendship resurrected in the wake of his injury. The secret of the house offer dances in the air between them; only now Ellie can push it out of her mind instead of letting it fester and invade her every thought.

Derek can still feel the anger rippling off Ellie towards him. Everyone else seems to be coming closer to each other but not to him. That's not the way it's supposed to be. His mind spins with ways he can turn things around. Becoming the hero could take a while; he'll need something else in the meantime. He needs something to glue them to him. "Um, so Thanksgiving is the week after next. You should be out way before then. How about we have dinner at my house that evening?"

"Yeah, okay." Whitney agrees, suddenly weirded out by his change in personality. Jackson nods. Derek turns to Ellie, his eyes big and apologetic. "How 'bout it, El? You know it won't be the same without you."

"Fine. Sure." She groans.

"Okay great. Well guys, I've got some stuff to do; let's give the man some rest." Derek claps a hand on Jackson's shoulder, before turning to the door.

"Yeah, I need to bring Mel home. I'll be back tomorrow, okay?"

Not knowing what to say, Ellie leans forward giving Jackson a gentle hug, cautious of his ribs.

"You'll come back too, yeah?" He asks.

"You got it." Ellie nods and makes her way to the door, breezing past Derek, and out into the hall. Feeling the need for some space, she keeps walking, not bothering to wait on her friends. She hits the button for the elevator and hurries in, letting the doors slide closed just as Derek and Whitney step out of Jackson's room.

24

A long line of people wait at the ticket stand as Ellie walks up to the movie theater. Instead of letting James pick her up, she insisted they meet here. Definitely interested in James, but still worried about Jackson, she didn't feel up to bringing him around her family. Not yet anyway. Her parents will like him, of course, but thanks to Derek, she's had her fill of other people's opinions on the date. She wants to make her own opinions first. *Who is he to judge?* She hasn't been in Derek's life for a long time. He has no right to have a say on who she does or doesn't spend her time with. Thoughts of her argument with Derek bring her mood down, and she wants to have a good time tonight, so she sets her shoulders back, pastes a smile on her face and looks around in search of James.

There he is, and the sight of him dissolves any anger she carries instantly. James, standing by the door and looking excruciatingly handsome in his tan corduroy jacket and dark jeans, spots her and waves. He looks warm, and she can't wait to be inside the dim theater and out of the cold. Shivering a little in her peach sweater dress and wedges, she rushes over, careful not to trip in her heels.

"Hi." She breathes out a puff of cold air.

"It's good to see you again." He leans in, his lips just barely grazing her cheek. "I got our tickets. They're showing classics in the back theater—there's a Lauren Bacall double feature. You like her, right?"

"I love her!" Ellie bounces on her feet for warmth. "How did you know?"

"I may have checked your social media." He laughs, dipping his head.

Her face drains of color; noticing, he rushes to explain. "I didn't want to plan something you wouldn't like. I just got lucky this event is tonight."

"Oh, okay." She tells herself to stop being weird; they are Facebook friends after all. This guy's not a creep. He just wants her to have a fun night. *Connor would never have gone to the trouble for me.* Relaxed and smiling, although still shivering in the cold, she slips her hand through his arm. "Well, let's go; we wouldn't want to miss anything. I wonder what's playing. I hope it's Dark Passage—that's my favorite, you know."

Chuckling, he escorts her inside, his hand sliding to the small of her back as he drops her arm to open the door. "Well, then this works out great. It's Noir Night—Dark Passage, and The Big Sleep." He mashes his lips together dramatically and winks, doing his best Bogart impersonation.

Feeling lighter than she has in a long time, Ellie laughs. "You do a perfectly awful Bogie."

Laughing, he lifts her hand, twirling her around amongst all the movie-goers moving around them, and all she feels is magic.

They're early, so they have their pick of the seats. They take the stairs and make their way up choosing Ellie's favorite spot—just higher than halfway and seated in the middle. There's a smattering of other classic lovers here and there, but mostly they're alone. Ellie shivers in the low-lit room.

"Here, take my jacket." James shrugs it off and slides the jacket around her shoulders. "Better?"

"Better." She nods. "Thank you."

"I'm going to go grab us some popcorn. Is there anything else you would like?"

"Oh, skittles!" She blushes.

"Skittles it is." He fusses with the jacket around her for a moment before taking off in search of their snacks.

Settling back into her seat, Ellie can't help but to smile to herself. *James really grew into himself.* You would never know that he used to try so hard; now, everything about him seems effortless. With his lean runner's form, wavy blonde hair, and light brown eyes, he has grown up gorgeous. She chides herself for focusing so much on his looks, but deep down, she knows that's a big reason that she's here. When they were teens, she couldn't be bothered to ever give him the time of day. Rolling her eyes, she thinks of the old, giant glasses that never seemed to fit his face.

A draft blows through the old theater, and she nestles deeper into the soft corduroy, sliding her hands into the pockets. Her fingers graze something, thin and rectangular, it feels like a business card. Before she can pull it out to look, James saunters back up the aisle toward her, loaded down with sodas, popcorn, and skittles. She grabs the drinks from his hands, helping him unload their snacks, the card in the pocket completely forgotten.

The screen flares to life, and drawn to it, Ellie pulls her gaze from James. Instead of movie previews, black and white cartoons play on the screen filling her with a nostalgia for her childhood carefree weekend mornings with her grandparents.

Leaning in and whispering, James interrupts her memory. "Thanks for coming tonight. I'm so glad I ran into you the other day."

"Yeah, I'm glad too." Feeling almost shy, she looks at him through her lashes.

"It's crazy right? I wanted to ask you out so many times in high school, but I always chickened out." He holds the greasy bag of popcorn out to her.

"Oh?" Embarrassed, she focuses on the popcorn so that she doesn't have to look him in the eye. He wouldn't have liked her answer back then. "You should have."

"Yeah right. Ellie Meechum, you lie." He chuckles, before coughing. "You would never have gone out with me, and besides, you and your friends were an impenetrable force."

Canned laughter from the old cartoon on screen

loudly forces its way into their conversation, taking her attention for a moment. Glad for the tiniest distraction, she takes a moment to breathe, feeling a little cornered. "Well, you're right. I didn't do much without my friends. I didn't have any siblings, so they kind of made up for that. But, I did date outside of the group, mostly in college, though."

"Oh, that's right. You *were* with that long-haired guy. What was his name…Blake, was it?"

Dark soda splashes out of her cup as she drops it into the cup holder a little too forcefully. Whipping around to face James, tiny red flags pop up in her mind.

"What?" He elbows her shoulder playfully. "I went to the same college as you. I told you guys at the end of senior year, I'd be going there too, remember? I ran into Jackson one day on campus. He must've told you. No? You're looking at me like I'm crazy."

"No! Geez, I'm sorry. It seems like such a lifetime ago; I guess I don't remember. I mean; it makes sense though." Relief floods through her, along with a bit of self-consciousness as well.

After her last few relationships, it's almost impossible for her to trust a man, but she wants to try with James. It seems the tables have turned, and now, she's the one trying to impress him. Besides, it's not lost on her that he would run the other way if he knew how she lost it on Connor. The baseball bat and the pocketknife—he would never go near her again.

The lights lower further, and the swell of the ominous orchestra music immediately catches her attention as she turns to the screen to watch the opening credits of Dark Passage. She feels James's eyes on her, and distracted, she pulls her gaze from the screen, leaning in as he whispers in her ear.

"Look, I know I probably remember way too much about you, and I wasn't what anyone would consider 'cool' back then, I just always wanted friendships like what you guys had. I guess I was a late bloomer, I didn't really grow into myself until after college. This is so embarrassing, and you want to watch the movie--I'm sorry, I'm babbling. I'm just happy to be spending time with you, *really* getting to know you."

Completely charmed; Ellie smiles up at him. "I only wish I'd actually gotten to know you a long time ago."

"So do I."

But you didn't, and all it took was a complete physical transformation and the destruction of you and your friends' lives to make it happen. This time, he won't be taken in with her long legs and full lips. He won't allow her melodious laughter to call to him like a siren anymore. Smiling to himself, he throws an arm around her shoulders, and she leans in, nestling her soft hair into his neck. *Such a shame the movie doesn't end differently.*

PART TWO

25

His date with Ellie went well, not perfect, but good enough. If only he hadn't stuck his foot in his mouth that last time. Knowing her favorite actors was one thing, but bringing up Blake could've seriously backfired. He's got to learn to keep his mouth shut and listen more. It's his only downfall, he thinks. Regardless, she's still dying to see him again. It's a shame really; she's gorgeous, and knowing what he knows about her reaction to Connor—she seems like just his type of crazy. But, it took a complete change of appearance to get her attention, and besides, what can she do for him? Not much. No, she's not the one with any kind of power; that's Derek. He's the one with influence, and what does he do with it? Nothing.

Anyway, he'll just have to keep himself from falling for her. His memories will help with that. He'll keep seeing her, he decides. He has to, until their time is up. It's his only way in.

A smile creeps across his mouth as he thinks about the exhilaration he felt two nights ago. The run-in at the hospital couldn't have worked out better in regards to staying on everyone's radar. He'd watched; he'd known they were coming.

Landing the date was all a part of the plan, but getting to challenge Derek's alpha-male personality in front of Whitney and Ellie was icing on the cake. They took forever visiting with Jackson-it's not like he died, not yet, anyway. Just a couple broken bones, but you would've thought he'd landed in a coma the way Whitney was blubbering on. It's almost time, and he can't wait to wash the fakeness from their faces.

Relishing in his accomplishments he remembers every detail from their hospital run-in. The chips from the vending machine were greasy and stale, so he'd tossed them and kept moving, deciding it was better to wait at the entrance rather than down the hall. Poor Ellie left in a hurry; she must've had quite the argument with her friends. He watched as Whitney walked out, Derek following a few seconds after her, and it wasn't surprising. Of course, Derek would stay until everyone had gone to make sure they were all being good little friends doing exactly as they were told. He was the last to leave, so James hopped in his car and followed him. He kept several cars in between them; he already knew where to go, and he couldn't wait to see the look on Derek's face once he realized his client folders were no longer safely on his desk.

He'd brought the car to a crawl before stopping on the side of the road under a tree, just far enough from Derek's house that it wouldn't be noticed but close enough that he could jump in if needed. Because it's not time yet. Orange haze streaked across the sky as the sun began to set; he reclined his seat and leaned back, staring, he'd always loved sunset. The angry slashes of red and yellow daylight were fighting to keep control while the deep blues and blacks quietly overpowered them, drenching everything in darkness. Winning the battle slowly and completely. He gave Derek a few minutes to get settled inside, and he threw his arms behind his head, watching the oppressive night win its war.

Under the cover of a blue-black sky, scattered with stars, he crept behind a few houses, making his way through the dead, brittle grass to the only house at the moment that mattered. He'd smirked as he stalked past the singed shed, only wishing the whole thing had burnt to the ground. The point was made though. It didn't have to burn down; Derek just needed to see the fire to know that his secret wasn't very well kept. It seemed luck was on his side; the blinds were open and the light was on in Derek's bedroom. James slid carefully behind a row of holly bushes and peaked over the window ledge to watch as Derek whipped around his room, and dug through his desk in a frenzy, his facial expressions switching from anger to confusion before finally settling on the one that James came there to see: fear.

26

The missing client documents still have Derek shaken up; it's been two days since he'd noticed, but he can't let it go. Only those folders were missing; not one other thing had been touched, which could only mean that it was planned, not a random break-in. *But, how?* He could see how anyone could get past Moose—the dog never makes a sound, but the windows and doors were secure, nothing broken, and he always makes sure things are locked up before leaving. The only thing he can figure is the spare key taped to the inside of the birdhouse in a tree by the garage. He hasn't used the thing in months though; could someone have been watching him all this time?

He makes a note of it—he's taken to jotting down everything that's gone on since the day Ellie came back, and he learned the Doris house had sold. Bumping his knee on the kitchen table, he stands quickly, moving to the sink to pour his steaming coffee down the drain. His nerves are too frantic for caffeine.

His cell phone rests silently on the counter. He wants to call Ellie, to hear all about her date with that ridiculous James Myer. The guy has always been a loser; just because he looks different and grew some confidence doesn't make him any less lame. But he and Ellie didn't leave things on the best terms, and he doesn't want to make her any angrier than he has already. He hasn't spoken to her since leaving the hospital, but this is far more important. Maybe he could just call her, warn her about the break-in, make sure she's alright. After several minutes of deliberation, he decides to let it be. She won't want to hear from him right now. She's probably on high alert anyway after Jackson's "accident." She's the toughest to crack; it's usually best to give her some space.

Restlessness courses through his body—he should be leaving for work right now. Tuesdays are his in-office days. The chances of getting his job back are pretty much non-existent. It doesn't matter anymore; he's got to find out who did this to him—to all of them — and why. And he's also got to start looking for another place to work; he won't be receiving his last paycheck, and his mortgage and utilities are due soon. He grabs his laptop, once again taking his place at the table. But, where to start? He desperately needs another job—his savings won't pay for everything, but he's just had a burglary, and his best friend is in the hospital. It's only going to escalate. As he pulls up his resume, he notices the tremble in his hand—he's never been this out of control before and it terrifies him. Whoever broke in could come back at any moment; he should call the police. Shaking his head furiously at himself, he realizes that no, that won't do any good. They already think he was being dramatic about Jackson's injuries. If he starts going on about being robbed and the only thing missing is his folders, they'll go to his boss. He's almost positive that there will be a carefully laid trail pointing straight to him for the identity theft if he tries that. He can't be the hero from a jail cell.

All he wants to do is start working on figuring things out before someone else gets hurt, to end it so that he can be back on top, but his practical mind won't let him until he's tied up his loose ends. Quickly, he finds the file for his resume, adjusts a few things, then joins several job search websites, posting his credentials and hoping for someone to bite. Normally, he would put a little more thought into finding the right job, but he can't be bothered to waste hours of his life looking for the perfect fit. His resumes are out there—the right job is just going to have to find him.

Gazing out the window, Derek tries to understand what it is about the Doris house that has them all under this hold, almost as if they're hostages of the house without even being inside of it. *Could the house really be haunted?* He's never believed it before, and it makes no sense, why, after all this time, would a spirit bother to mess with them? Maybe the neighbors have something to do with it. But, he can't imagine their reasoning after all this time. And if they were targeting him and his friends they would have to target every other teenager that ever stepped through that door. Unless the neighbors were able to see inside the house and what he was about to do.

The clouds are low and heavy in the sky, pushing down around him, and the dark is setting in earlier these days. The peeling rocking chair on his back porch, a kitschy old hand-me-down from his mother, creaks with the electric tension in the evening air. A shudder rips through his body, he feels hateful stares coming from everywhere. He races to the window, closing the blinds, and overcome with paranoia, he checks the locks on all of the doors and windows in the house before once again sitting down to read over his notes.

By this point, he's practically memorized every word that's been written down, but there's this lingering feeling, something else that he needs to remember. His mind is too frazzled and his nerves too shot; he knows there's something he's missing, but he can't settle his mind to work through the puzzle. With a violent swipe, he clears the table of his notebook. Moose flinches as it hits the floor. His hands press down on the old wooden table top, and he glances wildly around the room. Zeroing in on his phone once again, that old feeling comes rushing back—much like the pull of a drug, only it's a different demon he's wrestling. He needs to know where Ellie and Whitney are, and he needs to get through to Ellie that he's the only one who can keep her safe, that he knows what's best for her. Him. Not that prick James.

He rushes to the counter and grabs his phone, scanning through his recent call list, but before he can press the button, it hits him. What he's been forgetting. He closes out of his calls and pulls up his phone gallery, studying the last photo he took. The photo of the Doris house. Moose lay at his feet, forgotten, as he zooms in and out, sliding the focus to every inch of the picture. But all there is, is the creepy old house and the **SOLD** sign lingering in the front corner. Useless.

No. Don't be that short-sighted. There's information to be found anywhere. Keep focused. A plan begins to take shape—if he can get ahold of the realtor, he can feign interest in another property and subtly ask a few questions about the house, maybe even find out who sold it, and who bought it. Gears turning in his mind, he slams his fist onto the countertop. No one makes a fool of him. He's got it. All he has to do is set up a meeting, get inside the realtor's office. If he can get a moment alone, he can look for paperwork or try to gain access to the computer and find out everything he needs to know about the house, including who lives next door. That information can provide some real clues as to who is stalking them. It's a long shot, but it's his only option.

Laptop and phone in hand, he rushes into the living room to get comfortable for investigating. Finally, he feels a purpose, something that can get this thing started. With a sigh, he reads through the boring Welcome section of the realtor's website before browsing a few of the listings. Not wanting to waste any more time, he pulls up the Meet Our Agents page to sift through the photos and bios of the agents. He's looking for the house's listing agent but still wants to size them all up in order to get his plan together. Bennett Turner. That's the agent he's searching for, but as he scrolls down, another name seizes the spotlight. Derek's hands fly from the computer as if he were burned. It teeters on the couch where it slid, and he stares at the picture on the screen, shocked. And as he stares into the cold eyes of James Myer, it begins to make sense. *Of course he is wound up in this. I knew something was off the minute I saw him. But what ties him to the Doris house? Or is it all simply because no one wanted to hang out with him?*

For just a moment, he's drowning. A wave of fear engulfs him completely. He can't tell the others yet; he needs to get facts first, proof of a connection. Something substantial. They're too enchanted with the new James. They'd never believe him. There's no doubt in his mind that James orchestrated everything: the accident, the fire, the snake and spiders, even Derek's job termination. He had popped right back into their lives at the perfect time. A new realization hits that terrifies him; if James hadn't wanted to be found out, he wouldn't be. *He's already prepared for this.*

27

"Are you sure you have your phone charger? Your toothbrush?"

"Whit, settle down. We have everything. You're the one who packed up, and you got it all. Just sit down and relax. The nurse will be here with the wheelchair soon."

Whitney takes a seat in the chair by the hospital bed but barely makes it all the way down before hopping right back up. "But I might have forgotten something. And maybe I should just go track down a wheelchair; she said she'd be back in five minutes. It's been nearly twenty." Whitney flits around, frantic and inspecting every aspect of the small room. "Oh, your discharge papers, I need those."

Jackson reaches out, straining, to grab her arm, giving her an encouraging squeeze. "Hey," he whispers. "We've got them. You put them in your purse when the doctor left, remember? It's okay."

"I know." Whitney sinks into the chair, tears in her eyes. "It's just, it seems safe while you're in here. There are so many people around. Once you leave, this thing continues. You're hurt, how can I protect you and Mel?"

"We'll be okay; we'll figure it out."

The clock by the door ticks out a calming rhythm as Whitney nods and sits back in silence, trying her best not to worry. Her head shoots up as the sounds of wheels squeaking across the tile floor and interrupting the pattern.

"Alright, Mr. Gray. Ready to get out of here?" The nurse is young, tall, and quirky with her cat eye glasses and soft green scrubs. She smiles warmly as she leans down to help Jackson off the bed and into the chair, gently laying his crutches across his lap. "You can go ahead and pull the car around. We'll meet you out front," she says to Whitney as she hooks his bag over the wheelchair handle.

"Oh, okay. Yeah, I'll see you down there."

The trunk is loaded; the nurse pushes the wheelchair back through the automatic doors of the hospital, and it's just Whitney and Jackson alone in the car. The bright morning sun shines in her eyes, and she squints, pulling down the visor before taking a deep breath and putting the car in drive. Back to reality. Back to whatever is lurking in the shadows.

"We'll stop by your house and get whatever you need, I'm sure you don't wanna keep wearing the same things you did in the hospital."

"That's okay, it can wait. You probably need to get Mel, huh?" He looks at her profile as she drives, grateful to be next to her, even under such awful circumstances. Whatever is going on, at least it brought Whitney back into his world.

"Oh, no. I spoke to her earlier; she's happy as can be at my mom's. She gets to have all the sugary treats she could want over there. I talked to my mom also; she's going to bring Mel home a little later tonight after we get you settled."

"That's nice of her. I guess I could use a few things. It'd be great to have some of my stuff with me while I'm not at home, and also I need to grab my computer. I've got some work calls to make."

"Oh my gosh, I hadn't even thought of that. What are you going to do about work? You can't be walking around lifting things right now." Taking her eyes off the road just for a moment, she glances down at the boot on his leg.

"Yeah, I'm going to see if I can get a couple of my temp guys out there to finish up what I've started. It's almost Thanksgiving. They should be on school break soon." He rubs his chin, wondering how much he trusts a couple of eighteen- and twenty-year-olds to complete the jobs correctly without him there. "And if they can't do it, I'll just have to let my customers know I'm injured. Shouldn't be too long before I'm back at it."

Whitney nods, driving the rest of the way in silent thought.

Lines of trees struggling to hold their brilliant, colorful leaves bleed into soft golden pastures. Jackson watches from the window at the cows scattered about, lazily grazing with none of the fear and anxiety that fills him up with dread.

Not once has he ever been nervous to return home, but as Whitney's car bounces up the gravel path, he starts to second guess things. His uninjured leg bounces on its own. As much as he's tried, he can't remember the fall, or the ride to the hospital. All he knows is that he for sure didn't dig any holes. Glancing down at the boot, he knows that he could deal with it by himself in his own home. As long as he isn't doing physically demanding work, he'd be okay. But, Whitney wants to help, and he wants to let her, and besides, he can't watch over her from his house. She steers the Camry up the path through the trees and the woods toward his house. It's a new feeling—this all-encompassing sense of intrusion.

"I'm so sorry," his hand rests on his sore ribs.

"For what?" The car idles for a moment before she turns it off and moves to face him.

The sun peeks through the clouds, giving Whitney an ethereal glow. The brisk wind whistles through the trees, and it's just the two of them in her car surrounded by all of the fiery red and orange colors of the season. It could almost be romantic. It could be perfect if they weren't being stalked.

"I didn't believe you guys. My rational side kicked in, and I just thought I could explain it all away, find a logical reason behind things, and I'm sorry. I feel so violated, and exposed and you guys must've been feeling this way the whole time, and I just didn't see it. The way that I just blew it off, I'm an idiot."

With a sigh, Whitney unbuckles her seatbelt and leans back. "Well, you believe us now, right?"

"Absolutely."

"Then let's just leave it behind us and try to keep ourselves safe while we figure out why this mess is happening."

"Deal."

"Now, let's get your stuff so you can get back to resting. What can I grab for you?"

If he goes, she'll be alone outside, and if she goes, she'll be alone inside, and whoever is after them might have no issues with coming back here, so he wriggles out of his own seatbelt and opens the door, struggling to stand up with his heavy boot. "We'll go together."

Quickly, Whitney moves around the car to put her arm around his back, helping to keep him steady as they make their way to his house. As they get to the porch, they turn to take in the scene; the deep and jagged hole, leaves scattered about, and a few scratch marks still imprinted in the dirt around the sides. As they walk past it, Jackson turns to look down into the hole where he could've suffered much worse. The sun chooses this moment to shine directly down onto him, illuminating the space, and he notices something partially hidden in the dirt there at the bottom. Careful not to trip in his boot, he releases himself from Whitney's grasp to peer down into the opening. There at the bottom of the hole lies a thin square of netting, perfect to scatter leaves over.

28

Seated at a secluded, rustic wooden table surrounded by grapevines, Ellie and James lean forward, clinking their glasses together. Their private wine tour now over, they sit, enjoying a nice little tasting. They laugh as the wine clumsily sloshes from the glasses. He may have filled them up just a little too much. James isn't a big drinker, and Ellie has yet to notice that he's been nursing the same glass since they sat down—though he is driving. Ellie is feeling light and carefree as she empties glass after glass, shedding her barriers and letting them float away like dandelions in the late afternoon breeze. A calming quiet settles over them as they both look out to watch the watery autumn sun wash over the rows and rows of grapevines. The land seems to stretch on forever.

Leaning back in his chair, James shoves both hands deep in his pockets, appearing relaxed and unbothered. His fingers fumble around the bottle of eye drops that he carries with him. He could do it—it would be so easy to just squirt a little into her glass when she goes to the restroom. There's no one else here, only the owners, and they're inside. But no, it's not time yet; it's not enough. She has to learn. They all do. And besides, he needs these eye drops for his eyes. The switch from glasses to contacts has not been an easy one for him, and he's more than ready to give up the red, itchy eyes in favor of his beloved glasses once more.

As if daring him to do it, Ellie stands gracefully and

excuses herself to the ladies' room. He watches on as she stumbles in her ridiculous heels up the path to the building. He didn't come this far to give in to temptation now, so he lets his grip on the bottle go and begins again thinking through his plan for her precious friends.

Ellie returns as the sun begins to make its descent, and good gracious, he thinks, she is radiant in this light. But such lovely things usually have horrible souls.

"Have I told you how beautiful you look today?"

Her cheeks redden as she sits, her blush a little deeper from the wine. "Yes, you have but thank you again."

"Well, should we move on to the next part of our night?" James stands, offering her his hand.

She takes it, eating the whole bit up. She loves how he speaks—so formal, so respectful. She wonders if he has always spoken that way; of course, she wouldn't know, having never bothered to listen to him before now.

They walk together down the path to the parking lot. He slides his arm around her waist so that he can steady her if she stumbles. *Maybe there's a chance.* But his eyes darken and swirl with years of pent-up hatred. No. He will not let himself go down that route; he won't let her win.

Lights shimmer and twinkle in the early night as they pull up to the local race track. Thanksgiving is not for a few days, but the speedway has already opened its Christmas lights drive-thru display. The two of them pull up, taking their spot in line, and as he finds their tickets on his phone, Ellie absentmindedly chats away. Only half-way listening, he hears her go on with something about how she missed things like this while she was living in Minneapolis.

Christmas music blares from outside, reverberating through the car. Ellie ignores the growing headache, forcing herself to stay focused and present on her date with James. The overly amplified sounds of tinkling bells fill her aching mind with static. Closing her eyes does little to stifle it, but her excitement overrides the discomfort. She still can't believe that she is actually happy to be here with him. She wonders if anyone else from school has seen the change in him. She can't contain how proud she feels to be the one that he chose to bring here tonight.

An elderly couple in the car ahead of him feels the need to stop completely to enjoy every display to the fullest, so after moving only a few feet, they sit, idling. Holding his phone down low near the driver's side door, he sneaks a glance at Ellie. She's staring out of her window. He pulls up an app, staring at the live video streams. It was a perfectly thought-out plan, installing tiny, imperceptible cameras outside of everyone's homes as they spent their time visiting Jackson in the hospital. Now, he can track all of their movements without having to physically drive from house to house for information. Nothing is going on outside of Derek's house, so he switches over to Whitney's cam. *There you are.* He watches her step out of her car, giant take-out bag in hand. He knows that Jackson is staying with her, which works out perfectly. Two birds, one stone, and all of that. Satisfied for now, he closes out his screen and turns back to Ellie who is still happily staring out at the lights. Finally; someone out of the growing number of cars behind him blows their horn, startling the older couple into moving at a better pace.

James masterfully hides his simmering rage and makes a compelling show of oohing and ahhing over the colorful Santa's workshop and the reindeer displays. He notices the rosiness of Ellie's face fade into a sickly white as they pull through the Land of Sweets. They drive into the flashing tunnel as if entering the world of Clara's dream while The Dance of the Sugar Plum Fairy echoes loudly around them. Bright, flashing lights of all colors bounce from every side. Ellie's vision glimmers in and out of focus, and she shuts her eyes to the swirling effect. Inhaling deeply, she tries to calm the wave of nausea that is cresting at the bottom of her throat. Inwardly, James laughs. Though he jokes to himself that he'll kill her if she throws up in his car.

"Hey, are you feeling alright?" Placing a hand on her arm, he looks at her, the very picture of concern.

"Oh, yeah," she lies. "This is amazing. I'm just feeling a little tired. I was up really early this morning."

"Ah. Well, I won't keep you out too late." He winks, giving her a wicked smile. "I'll take you home soon; it's almost over." He laughs and presses his foot down on the gas, catching up to the car in front. The strobe lights flare brightly and darken, revealing several rows of dark red and gold nutcrackers flashing to the beat. They exit the tunnel and pull out onto the highway, dark in comparison to the show, and he drives her home with all those glasses of wine sloshing in her stomach with every bump he hits. The roar of sudden silence fills both of their ears.

"Sorry about that., I shouldn't have had so much to drink today." She tries to make light of her situation.

"That's alright. I'm glad you had fun, I sure did. Don't worry, I'll get you home safe." And he will. For now. He's got other things to tend to.

29

It's late, but Derek couldn't just come home after that awful job interview. He needed to be around people, and everyone seems to be busy. At least his hastily posted resumes generated something, he thinks. Aside from the short call almost a week ago to let him know that Jackson was out of the hospital, he hasn't heard from any of his friends. No one has bothered to return his calls or messages. It's been years since he has been in the center of their circle, but how quickly the desire to keep his position has returned.

Not wanting to eat alone, he went to a little Mexican restaurant near his house, but watching all of the families and groups of friends enjoying their dinners together just made him feel worse. He ended up leaving with a box of half-eaten enchiladas and his confidence at an all-time low. He's certain he tanked the interview; he was fidgety and nervous, and once they check his past employment, the opportunity will officially be over. Maybe next time he should leave his previous job off the list. But that's not in his nature. If he can somehow get a couple steps ahead of James, he can prove his innocence. He won't be intimidated. He's already re-hid his spare key.

Moose is sound asleep in his bed in the living room, not even waking to greet him. Maybe he's taken for granted every other time that Moose trots to the door, happily panting and grunting, pawing at him for a snuggle. Tonight, he needs it the most.

Perhaps he's just being overly alert after everything that has happened, but something feels off. There's no lingering smell. Nothing is out of place, but it just *feels* off. Invaded space, like before. Frantic, he rushes from room to room checking, but no one is here, and nothing is out of place. Everything in his bedroom is just as it was this morning, same with his desk. He carries his restaurant leftovers to the fridge, chiding himself for his jumpiness and low attitude.

The phone in his pocket vibrates; he quickly pulls it out, hoping for a message from his friends, but it's only a weather alert. If someone would just call him back, he could let them in on his suspicions of James. Maybe they could all figure out a way to prove it because the guy is impossible to find anything on—none of Derek's time spent investigating has turned up anything other than where James works. Jackson wouldn't want to hear it though; they seem to be friendly after all. Ellie for sure won't listen, and of course, if Jackson and Ellie won't believe it, neither will Whitney. He's got to get his hands on something solid other than just the fact that James works at the same realty company that sold the house. Too upset to focus on digging up dirt tonight, he trades his leftovers for an unfinished sports drink and slinks off to his bedroom.

It's obvious they're upset with him—his friends. He needs to get them back on his side before mentioning anything about James, or they won't believe him. Hosting Thanksgiving is the best way to do that—he's already grabbed a turkey, stuffing mix, and potatoes. Everyone else will bring the rest. Thank goodness too because the turkey was way more than he wanted to spend now that he isn't working. Just one more day until he can try to make them understand.

The James of high school days comes to mind, and Derek realizes there's one more thing he can look into—old yearbooks. Maybe a school or band photo will unlock a memory or something. It's grasping at straws, but it's all he's got.

The faded blue plastic bin labeled Memorabilia

stays untouched and hidden at the bottom of his coat closet by the front door. With a longing look at the bed, he rushes out of the room to retrieve the bin. It's worth extending his miserable day to find something and end it with a win. He rips the lid off and dives into the contents, throwing old letters, tee shirts, and school assignments behind him as he digs. Finally, he finds four slender and shiny yearbooks. He looks through the dates, choosing the one from 11th grade first. James Myer is easy enough to find and he looks exactly like Derek remembers. He flips through the entire book page by page until he comes across an entire two page spread on the field day that year. Scattered across the pages are random photos of kids in all states of activity and relaxation on the football field. The photograph on the top right corner of the second page catches his attention. His lip curls in disgust as he rolls his eyes. A much younger group of himself, Jackson, Whitney, and Ellie sit on a beach blanket in the bright sun, laughing with pizza and sodas scattered around them. He remembers the picture, but what he didn't see at the time was the creepy, lanky kid standing awkwardly behind them, yogurt in hand and eyes laser focused on the back of Derek's head. James. Quickly, he rips the corner of an old assignment and shoves it into the book, marking the page and setting it aside to go through the rest.

The 9th and 10th grade yearbooks offer nothing more than a class photo of James. Regardless of the clubs and teams he attempted to join, he doesn't exist on any of their pages. Jumping to the school band's picture, he finds a boring photo of James in a performance hat, entirely too big for his young face. With a yawn and a deep stretch, Derek releases some tension before cracking open another book—senior year. He's starting to think there's nothing to find in this one as well until he reaches the back of the yearbook—the senior pages, the ones parents purchase to embarrass their kids with ridiculous photos from their childhood. There's a half page spread for James from his mother. Swallowing the bile rising in his throat, he blinks, making sure what he sees is really there. It is. His stomach lurches with a sour mix of righteousness and horror. He certainly found what he was after. There will be no denying this, he thinks, as he marks the page and packs the box with everything but the two yearbooks he needs. Carrying them back to his room, he sets them on the dresser. Disgusted but satisfied, he's ready for a hot shower and some sleep.

His tee-shirt hits the side of the laundry basket and bounces off as he tosses his clothes across the room. He slides on some gym shorts before heading to the bathroom to brush his teeth. Hidden under the cover of the night's darkness, James watches everything from the other side of the window.

The room glows with the soft light from his table lamp, and Derek restlessly flops around in his bed, wishing Moose wasn't in the other room. Just another of his companions that seems to not need him. Frustrated, he sits, chugs from his drink, and grabs his phone. That out-of-control feeling has been building steadily for a few days now, but today, with the failed interview and lack of contact from his friends, it grows stronger than ever. With so much built up, it's almost painful. He needs to know what is going on with his friends. He has to know. Not expecting a reply but giving it another shot anyway, he shoots a quick text to Whitney.

Hey what're you guys up to.

Overcome with sudden exhaustion, he nestles into the pillows, falling into a deep sleep. The phone drops from his grasp onto the thick carpet.

With great satisfaction, James backs away from the window, scraping his arm on the bush as he goes. He keeps to the grass on his way back to his car so as not to disturb anyone with his footsteps. The only sound is the slight rattle of the sleeping pills clinking together in his pocket. Victorious, he can't wait for the next part of his plan. The one thing he hadn't counted on was Derek seeing the senior page. James had forgotten it was even in the yearbook, but now that Derek knows his little secret it will make what comes next even sweeter.

From the floor of Derek's bedroom the phone lights up with a reply from Whitney.

Hey! Sorry I haven't had a chance to get back to you. It's been super busy here with Mel and Jackson. Everything's good though, haven't heard a peep from our little friend since the accident. Maybe it's over?

30

"Another text?" Jackson slides the pillow up under his back, making himself more comfortable on Whitney's old, worn-in, light blue couch. Slivers of moonlight shine through the gauzy curtains, highlighting his face in such a glow that Whitney has to tear her eyes from his irresistible features.

"Yeah, but I answered this time." She turns, making herself busy by gathering up the wrappers and soda cups and smashing them deep inside of the greasy take-out bag. She walks it to the trash can in the kitchen, more for a breather than a need for tidiness, before she comes to rest on the couch beside Jackson.

"This time? You haven't spoken to him yet?"

"No, have you?"

"I called him when I was released."

"That was last Thursday! You can't get onto me about it if you're not talking to him either. Besides, I just texted him back, I told him we've been busy."

"Yeah, busy hiding out."

Whitney rolls her eyes. "We're not hiding out; I'm only taking time off from work to help you with your leg. Anyway, I'm still taking Mel to school and to all her stuff; it's not like I'm not leaving the house or anything. It's just, I don't know. I got this weird feeling from Derek at the hospital like how he kind of spun out with all the planning and pushing and trying so hard after that night. Do you remember? I can't explain it, just like he's not himself. It felt strange again, the way that he was talking. I think I needed a little space from the friendship if that makes any sense. Besides, whoever was doing this stuff seems to have gotten what they wanted because nothing's happened since your accident."

"No, I know." He grabs one of Melody's pencils from the coffee table, sliding it under his boot to scratch his itching leg. "He did get weird for a while after being in that house, like he was really spooked or something. He was so clingy and then out of nowhere he just dropped us. But I don't necessarily think that's what's happening here."

"Really, then why haven't you talked to him? I mean, he's the one who found you. Who knows how long you could've been knocked out for, or…?" Her voice cracks and she quiets when she sees the fear in his eyes.

"That's just it. *I'm* the one who got hurt here. I'm afraid too. I'm not Derek, okay? I don't want to go digging things up, not when you're involved. It's too risky. And I just…. haven't felt like talking to anyone about it. I haven't wanted to talk to anyone at all, I mean, besides you."

His rough and calloused hand clasps hers. She looks down at their hands, having lost all of her former bravery with her feelings. Gently, she squeezes his hand before letting go and standing. Lately, it's becoming a never-ending back and forth with her emotions. She felt ready at the hospital. There was no issue showing how she felt, but now that he's out, and in her house, it all feels too much. She can't help but to stuff it back down.

"I get it, I really do, but you're running out of time. His dinner thing is the day after tomorrow; that is, if you still want to go?"

"Yeah," he nods. "We should still go."

"Well, it's late. I'd better go check on Mel and head off to bed myself. Do you need any help getting to your room?"

"Nah, if you could just hand me those, I'll be fine." He nods toward the bookcase.

"Oh, of course." Two wooden crutches lean against

the old build-it-yourself bookcase, and she grabs them, helping him to get off the couch and situated with them. "Okay, well, if you need anything else, let me know." With an awkward side-hug that heats the base of her neck with embarrassment, she turns to the short hallway heading towards Melody's room to peek in.

"Goodnight," he calls, smirking at her retreating figure over the way she meticulously side-stepped her feelings. He'd never seen her as anything more than a good friend—a best friend, until they went to college. It was okay though, he could avoid it and they were seeing other people. He never let on until the night they went into the house. The dark, exhilarating night, and the way she looked at him—the charade was over. He could no longer tamp it down. Then his feelings became complicated; everything was complicated. And now, after years of forgetting, she's thrust back into his life, and neither of them can seem to figure out how to articulate what it is that they want. Back then, the group was falling apart. Now, everyone is trying to heal old wounds amidst an unseen danger. With a heavy sigh, he wonders if their timing will always be off.

The guest room is small and dark—if you can even call it a guest room. It's more the size of a home office or very small den. A tiny, white-walled room, with a full-size bed, a nightstand, and an empty sliding closet. No attached bathroom, but he doesn't mind having to hobble down the hallway. It's a nice change for him to be in a home with other people, and life, not just surrounded by the woods. The quiet that the woods provide is something that he loves, but he's finding more and more that he loves the fun and silliness of being with Whitney and her daughter even more.

Since there is no dresser, his bags lay messy and open at the foot of the bed while his laptop and notebooks rest next to a skinny lamp on the nightstand. He powers up the computer and glances over tomorrow's schedule. A couple of senior guys from the high school agreed to finish up the open jobs, and the clients all seem pretty satisfied so far, except for Mr. Walker. It's no surprise that he would be the difficult one. His phone call with the older man was brief; he was told in no uncertain terms that Mr. Walker would rather wait for him to be back up and running and finish what he started. Mr. Walker didn't want any "young kids" traipsing through his yard. So that was that. Everything except Mr. Walker's yard would be finished on time, and any new clients will go on a wait list until the boot comes off.

Satisfied with the way his business is running along without him, he closes the computer, hefts himself onto the bed, and loosens the straps on his boot before leaning back, arms behind his head. The ache in his leg serves as a non-stop reminder of the horror movie that his normal life has become. He stares up at the dated popcorn ceiling and wonders who outside of these walls hates him and his friends enough to do the things that have been done to them.

Memories of people and experiences from that time in his life run their course through his mind. It couldn't have been Shelby—his old college girlfriend. He was dating her at the time they went to the house, and he did eventually tell her about his hooking up with Whitney. Sure, she was angry, but that was then. She has a family now, husband, kids, the whole thing. She's never seemed to be the type to hold onto past hurts. Now, Adam, Whitney's old boyfriend, was a big guy, intimidating and tough. Jackson never spent much time around him. All he knew was that he was dating Whitney, and he played baseball. But, he isn't sure if Whitney ever even told Adam what happened. If she did, he was never made aware of it. Adam got a baseball scholarship not long after and transferred schools and Jackson never really heard her mention him again. And surely none of their exes would want to hurt *all* of them. It feels too extreme. What would Adam or Shelby have against Ellie and Derek?

Wonder if the place really could be haunted? The bed squeaks as he shifts his weight, shaking his head— embarrassed of even thinking it. Then again, he remembers the leg. He ran past it so quickly, but he definitely saw it, *or saw something* on the way out. *Maybe it's not such a strange thought. What if all of those kids with their ghost stories were right? Or maybe, the leg belonged to a murder victim. Someone may think we saw something that we didn't. Could someone have been killed moments before we snuck in? It makes sense why the threats are happening now. With the house being sold and remodeled, the killer could be making sure we don't talk.*

Dark brown and yellow bruises color the area of his leg above the boot. He stares at his own legs and feet for a long time in the quiet. A hard knot sinks in his stomach as it dawns on him, his leg. That's his connection to the Doris's house; someone or something knows that he was the one to see the leg. His fall couldn't have been anything other than intentional. He runs through every single thing that his friends have experienced since it all began, and he comes to a conclusion; each incident has either been to remind them of the house or to absolutely terrify them. Someone knows they were there and what they were doing, and if they know about him and Whitney and that he saw a person's pale leg in that abandoned room, then what do they know about Derek and Ellie? Most likely the spiders were a scare tactic and she's holding onto what really happened to her.

Had he truly listened to them the day they came to his house, he might have avoided this whole ordeal. They all need to come together and just spill it, let everything be out in the open. That's going to be the only way they can see the whole picture. He snatches his phone lying by his side, ready to fire off a couple of texts but stops short. Nothing else has happened to Whitney or him in the past few days. Ellie would have rushed over if anything happened to her, and Derek's been calling, but Derek is always calling. If it really has stopped, then maybe leaving it alone would be the best idea. Better not to poke the bear.

31

All of a sudden, it's starting to feel like Ellie and her friends are back to who they once were. Back to the days before the house when they actually liked each other. At first, when she left the hospital, she was so angry at Derek that she was sure she wanted to cut ties. Not even with just him, she was ready to be done with all of them for good this time. But she forced herself to do something new—something she didn't do in Minneapolis or any other time in her life. She decided to swallow her pride and take some time to really think about her relationships. It would be silly to throw it all away over a stupid argument. She's quick to take up a grudge, but she's learning to be just as fast at letting it go. Minneapolis was amazing, but lonely; all she really had was Connor, and her job, and neither turned out so well. She didn't even want to speak to Whitney a few weeks ago in the restaurant, and now, she's realizing what she was missing for so long was that cozy feeling of belonging in her group of friends. It doesn't matter where she falls in their hierarchy; she just wants to be in the circle without all the anger and resentment.

Feeling her pessimism begin to fade, she zips up her favorite gray Sherpa jacket and slides into her car. The heater blasts full force, and she lets the engine warm up as she shivers and blows on her hands in an attempt to stifle the cold. After a few minutes, the car grows warmer and she relaxes her posture, leaning over the seat to dig around her purse for her phone. Her message notifications light up the screen—a new text from James. She huffs with annoyance; of course, she's happy to hear from him, it seems they are texting constantly these days, but she was really hoping for a response from Derek.

Thanksgiving is tomorrow, and he insisted on hosting a dinner for the four of them at his house. At first, she was dreading it, and besides, she'll already have eaten with her family, but after spending so much time with James and remembering how he went through his younger days alone, it's made her so grateful for her friends, even Derek. She's actually a little bit excited about it now. He's probably mad that she waited so long to return his texts so he's ignoring her. It's not like she meant to avoid him all week. She just needed time. But now, she's been calling and texting all morning and nothing. He may be even more aggravated when he finds out she's wanting to know if she can invite James along, but Derek is someone you need to feel out before something like that, so she's been leaving messages to see if there's anything else he needs her to bring that's not on the list he's already provided. *Maybe I'll just bring him anyway.* A wicked smile spreads across her face—sure, she's trying to change, but seeing Derek's reaction would be well worth the steps back. He's just making some ridiculous power-struggle when there isn't one. She switches on her music and tosses the phone on the passenger seat; he's probably still out there playing detective, she assumes, even though things have calmed down since Jackson's injury. It's his own fault if he doesn't get back to her, so she'll bring James and maybe an extra dessert.

Eyes closed right where she stands, Ellie takes a couple deep breaths in the middle of the crowded bread aisle of the grocery store. Feeling stupid for not realizing that the day before Thanksgiving is the worst time to be here, she desperately tries to quell the growing frustration from watching all of the other shoppers bump into each other and rush around to clear the shelves. For a brief moment, she envisions what it would be like to just ram her cart straight down the aisle, grabbing whatever she needs without saying 'excuse me' or waiting for anyone to move out of the way.

The image doesn't gel with her newfound Zen, but it does make her giggle a little, and it relieves some stress so she can finish shopping.

After an excruciatingly long wait to check out and a promise to herself not to ever make this mistake again, Ellie pushes her cart to her car, happy to be done with the task, regardless of the hours lost. She pulls her sunglasses down, throws her long hair behind her, and tears off out of the parking lot, not noticing the figure watching her from the car two rows over.

She barely manages to look both ways before making a right turn onto the highway, heavy on the accelerator, moving faster until she's well above the speed limit. Careless, fast. The Mazda shakes a little, then swerves to the left. Ellie grapples with the steering wheel, trying to stay in the lines, then she hears the pop, and that unmistakable sound of scraping as the metal of her wheel meets the road. The car starts to fishtail as she reminds herself to ease up on the brakes. Slamming on them will only make it worse.

"Are you kidding me?!" She yells to no one, turning on her hazard lights and guiding the car to the shoulder. She slaps the steering wheel in anger, throwing her new easy-going attitude out the window. There's almost no need to look; she knows the tire is shredded. And as she reaches for her phone to call for help, a car pulls up behind her honking its horn. Not wanting to be bothered by some random passerby, she glares into the rearview mirror, daring someone to cross her. Only it's not just some holiday traveler; it's James. Relief courses through her, and she eagerly rolls the window down. *Thank God.*

"Got a spare?" She shrugs, putting the damsel-in-distress bit on thick.

"Uh, no actually. I used it a while back, forgot to replace it. Don't you?" He leans his arm on the hood of her car, peering in at her, as cars rush by alongside of them.

"Nope. Bought it used from the owner. It didn't come with one, and I guess I just kept putting it off." Her eyes lower, sheepish under his intense gaze.

"Well, we'd better go get one then." He turns to give

her space to step out, stopping as she calls out.

"I can't! Not right now, anyway. I've got deli casseroles and pies in the back for Thanksgiving. I need to get this stuff in the fridge."

"Okay, let me just look at the tire really quick. I might be able to patch it. If not, I can take you home and go grab you a tire while you do your stuff."

"Are you sure? You must have somewhere to be right now? I don't think the tire can be saved."

"Nah, it's fine." He leans down, running a hand along what's left of the wilted tire, inspecting every inch while Ellie gets out of the car and stands next to him. "Here's the problem." He motions to the tire. "You've got a gash right here." He slides his finger along the slices of torn rubber, eliciting a small chuckle.

"Just a little one, no big deal." She laughs.

"What in the world did you drive over? A mirror?" He smiles at her and stands, dusting his hands off on his jeans, charming her with every move.

"I have no idea!" She groans.

"I'll just move a few things out of the way, and we can move your stuff to my car. Sound good?"

"Sounds great, thanks."

With a smile plastered across his face, he walks back to his car, quickly grabbing the pocketknife from the cup holder and throwing it into the glove box. This was worth sitting in that stupid parking lot for two hours, he thinks. *I ruined her day and saved it all at once.*

James, ever the outward gentleman, grabs the paper bags from Ellie's grasp. "I've got a lot of work stuff in my trunk, so we'll need to throw these in the backseat."

"That's fine."

"After I get your tire fixed, I'll come get you and take you back to your car. That alright?"

"That would be amazing, thanks." She grins, slumping down comfortably in the passenger seat, grateful that he happened to drive by when he did.

All the lights are on as the two of them pull into Ellie's parent's driveway. He shuts the car off and rushes around the side to open the door for her, giving her his hand to help her out. Every detail is critical. He hefts the grocery bags into his arms, walking behind her, up the path to the front door.

"Looks like your folks are home."

Ellie glances at the front door, then back to James. "Yeah, they are. Would you want to come inside and meet them, just for a minute?"

He purses his lips, in effort to hide the smile that wants to creep its way across his mouth. "Yes, I think that'd be nice."

Rummaging in her purse for her key, she turns quickly back to him, nearly knocking the bags out of his hands. "James?"

"Yeah?" He shifts the bags effortlessly to his side.

"Do you have any plans for tomorrow night?"

32

The phone buzzes softly in the carpet, yet to be retrieved from where it landed last night. It jitters this way and that as texts from Ellie pour in one after another. A long slop of drool falls out of Derek's mouth onto the pillow while the early afternoon sunlight beams through his open blinds. From across the street, a leaf blower roars to life finally stirring Derek from his drugged haze. Carefully, he extends his arms behind himself to sit up, but the pounding pressure in his head proves too much, and he tumbles off the bed, making it to his toilet just in time to vomit.

After a long while of sweating and gagging on the floor, he's able to stand and wash up. He feels hungover, but he hadn't had a drink last night. He ate at one of his favorite places and then came home. *Probably food poisoning.* But, if it was, he would still be sick, and he's starting to perk up a bit except for the dehydration headache. Reasoning that he must have just caught a quick bug, he trudges to his closet to find some clothes.

"Moose! Wanna go outside?" He calls out, making his way up the hallway looking for the dog. "Moose!" He stops cold when he sees Moose laid out on his old dog bed in the living room. Moose is normally up with the sun and pawing at him, begging to go outside. Derek glances at the clock on the wall. One in the afternoon. He's slept half the day away! He rushes to Moose's side just as the little dog groans and stretches his paws straight out. Moose rights himself and jumps up, racing toward the backdoor.

"Oh, thank God." Derek breathes a sigh of relief. "What's gotten into us, Moose?" He stares out of the bay window in the kitchen, watching Moose scamper around the yard in search of the perfect spot to relieve himself.

The fog clears from Derek's mind once that first cup of coffee hits his throat. "It's Wednesday!" He yells to no one, banging his forehead with his fist. The plan was to get up early and get a head start getting the house ready for tomorrow night's dinner party. There's so much still to be done. Aside from all of the cleaning, he needs to set the table, prep the food, reset the coffee maker, and come up with a gentle way to break the news about James. He certainly can't just shove the yearbooks in their faces; he has to be smart about it. He'll have to tell them in such a way that they will listen, especially Ellie. She'll most likely already be on the defense. He debates which yearbook to show them first. If he shows them the field day picture, they may brush him off and not bother looking at the house photo. But showing them the house picture first allows no build-up. He needs the ultimate unveiling in order to come out on top, to be the one who solved it and the one who can stop it.

Moose scratches at the door, snatching him away from his internal panic. Quickly, he pours the dog's food from a large canister, leaving Moose to his breakfast while he goes to his room to search for his phone. He nearly trips over it rushing to his nightstand to look.

Sitting down on the bed, he turns the screen on, ready to pull up his notes app to start checking things off his list. But when the screen comes to life, he is shocked and thrilled to find more than a dozen missed calls and texts from his friends. His excitement is cut short when he realizes that something might be wrong if they are trying this hard to get ahold of him. *Or maybe they really do need me.* There are two texts from Whitney, one from Jackson—sent late last night, and all of the rest are missed calls and texts from Ellie asking about Thanksgiving food. He lies back on the bed, so happy that nothing major seems to have happened and that everyone is over their anger with him and moved on. They must have been worried about him to have called so much. If only he hadn't slept so late, he wouldn't have missed it. *But it might actually be a good thing; they'll be more receptive if they've been worried about me. I'll text them back later.*

The stylus clicks out of its place in the phone, and he scrolls over his list, adding things and checking others off as he goes. There's no more time to waste so he stands; overcome with a wave of dizziness, he leans against the bed for support. His stomach growls, he should probably eat something after being sick, but right now, there are things that need to get done. He'll eat later, he decides.

An hour later; the bathroom is clean, and the living room has been dusted and vacuumed to perfection. He grabs a shopping bag from the coat closet and unloads the sparse decorations that he bought. A few cinnamon and apple scented candles in deep purples and reds look nice scattered throughout the space. The rest of his purchases are leaf-printed napkins and brown cutlery, so he tosses the bag on the table and leads Moose out the door to gather some firewood to bring inside. Once the logs are neatly stacked in their holder next to the fireplace, he stands, taking a sweeping look around the room. For the first time since buying this house, the living room really looks cozy, ready to be filled with people. He can picture it; himself standing by the fireplace in his nice wool sweater and dark jeans, telling a joke, or story, perhaps as Whitney, Ellie, and Jackson all look up at him from where they're sitting with awe in their eyes and smiles on their faces, completely captivated. And once he brings out the yearbooks, the truth will be made clear and they will be so grateful for his troubles. It's going to be perfect.

All that's left is to handle the kitchen, so he pulls up his favorite playlist on his phone, turns the volume up, and begins clearing the counters. There's plenty of room for everyone to set up their food, and the area around the coffee maker is now all neatly put together with mugs, stir sticks, sweeteners, and a small variety of flavored syrups. For a moment Derek's so excited that he considers pulling out his boxed Christmas tree—it would be so festive. But no, it's too early for that, and besides, evening is settling in, and he still needs to set the table and grab some dinner. Tomorrow, he wants to get the turkey in the oven early so he can sit back and watch some football before everyone arrives.

Once the table is set, he places the last candle in the center and admires his handiwork. "What do you think, Moose? Not bad, huh?" Moose's nails skitter across the kitchen floor as he comes to stand by his owner, looking longingly at his food bowl. "Alright, alright. Dinner time."

After feeding Moose, Derek grabs a frozen meal from his freezer and pops it in the microwave. He stands at the fridge looking over the drinks neatly organized inside. He wants to save most of them for tomorrow, so he grabs a bottle of water at the top, and carries his food to the living room. The last thing he wants to do is have to reset the table. The t.v. serves as background noise as he devours his food. As he grabs his water, he notices the seal is broken. *Probably just got it out last night and changed my mind.* He guzzles the cold water, washing his food down, and savors the fact that he won't have to eat alone tomorrow.

Feeling on top of the world, he leans back, satisfied and proud, and back in control. With a start, he remembers the texts from everyone. Snatching his phone off the coffee table, he throws his feet up and starts to reply to Ellie. Only, before he can finish the text, the room begins to swirl. He blinks slowly, a thought at the back of his mind tugs at him; he shouldn't be seeing two of everything. But he's too tired to listen to it. The dizziness won't shake, and he can't remember why he's holding his phone, so he drops it at his side and turns to lie on the couch as his eyes close. The last thing he sees is the back of his eyelids as he is thrust into a deep sleep.

33

From somewhere up in the trees, an owl hoots, interrupting the early morning silence. The sun has yet to rise, but he's up. It's been weeks of preparation, and there's still much to be done. He's thought about it for years but never imagined he would actually be able to get the whole group back together, but now that Ellie's returned home, it's all working out. It couldn't have fallen into his lap at a better time. His watch glistens by candle light; 6:15 A.M. It's going to be a long day, but it'll all be worth it. He takes a heavy slug of his coffee, slams the mug down on the countertop, and smiles. It's Thanksgiving. And what is he thankful for today? Opportunity. Reunions. Revenge.

Will this heal his scars? He doesn't know, but it'll be fun to find out. Derek, Ellie, Whitney, and Jackson, the names roll through his brain on repeat. There are lessons to be learned today. They went into that house wanting a haunting, so that's what they're going to get. James pulls a folded picture out of his pocket, staring at it for a long while, only putting it back once the muted morning light shimmers through the blinds. It's going to be a beautiful day. He hangs the last sound-proof curtain and stands back to admire his work. By the end of the day, they are going to know who he is.

The house is old, built in the mid 1940's. A rambling farmhouse complete with all the trimmings of its time: basement, living room and den, grand foyer, a large ornate dining room, and a bathroom with hot water and a flush toilet. A luxurious home on beautiful land was all the owners wanted after recovering from the great depression. But beauty tends to fade, and eventually, the lovely white paint tarnished and chipped, the shiny metal fence rusted, and the oak tree in the front yard grew wild and twisted, casting its shady branches out wide, blocking light and dousing the home in shadows. As the years marched on, the once dreamy, sun-soaked home transformed, and with that transformation, came all of the makings of a legendary haunted house.

With his eyes closed, James remembers coming here as a very young child before he was old enough to hear the rumors. Running through the backyard and climbing to the top of the plum tree to sneak a sweet treat from the top branches. Exploring the rooms indoors to find just the perfect secret hiding spot. No matter what anyone else says about the house, to him it has always been magical. He thought he could let it go, but when his uncle put it back on the market, he couldn't bear to be the one to sell it. After he heard about the offer from Jackson, he knew it had to be his. There was no way he would let *him* have it. Ellie blowing up her life in Minneapolis and running home, tail between her legs, was the icing on the cake. He really should thank her, after all her return set the plan in motion.

The neighbors next door are far enough away to not hear anything, but you can never be too careful, so he went with soundproof curtains for the walls—he'll renovate after. Luckily Mr. & Mrs. Rodingham are out of town for the holiday—that's the only downside to the place, her constant curtain twitching. He wonders what might've happened if she hadn't called the police all those years ago. The cops never saw him though, he thinks with pride. By then, he'd already been hiding in the bushes for so long he became unnoticeable as he followed them inside. Growing up without any friends, he'd learned young all of the ways to go undetected. If the house had burned…well, he doesn't like to think about that.

He picks up a permanent marker from the counter and throws it into a drawer before grabbing the phone resting inside, composing a quick group text. He glances at the time at the top of the screen; 8:00 A.M. *It's time*. In swift motion, he hits the send button, shuts off the screen, and slides the phone into his back pocket before carefully blowing out the candle. From the opposite pocket, he pulls the creased picture back out, straightens it reverently, and walks through the living room to place it on top of the mantel. Perfect. Now, he just has a few more things to take care of.

As he passes by the old dining room, he stops, looking around at all the dust and debris. The light fixture fell ages ago yet still lies shattered and twisted on the table, little bits of glass scattered all around. Angry slashes of spray-painted graffiti cover the once beautiful curio that housed all of the expensive china. Now, those pieces of blue toile dishes lay all over the room, broken, never to be used for a special Christmas dinner again. He knows who did it—who destroyed the room. The girl whose anger was unleashed. The leg was meant for her, after all. He'd rushed in moments before they arrived, placing it in a spot they were all likely to be near, hoping that she would be the one to see it. He could hear her screams in his mind. He wanted to frighten her the most. By a stroke of luck, she did end up in the dining room, but because of her rage-filled tantrum, she didn't notice it. But Jackson did. Settled behind the dark curtains of the big picture window, James watched as Jackson ran past, doing a terrified double-take as he spotted the realistic looking mannequin leg. The fake blood had been a spur of the moment addition but a great one. Really, a stroke of genius.

Just off the living room is the private den. In the past, his young eyes saw it as a mysteriously dim-lit grown-up room. What it actually was, was an office for working hours and a clubhouse of sorts for the male guests to get away for a poker game or three after a hard day. This room held such fascination for him; so, it's the only fitting spot for the one who intrigues him the most. The imposing cherry wood door sticks a little, warped by the years and the ever-changing weather. With a hearty shove, he ambles into the room, a mere ghost of its former glory. The magic is in the memories now. The burgundy paint on the walls has faded and sprouted a sheen of dust, the card table lay broken and upturned, and the rich leather chairs that at one time sat before the elegant desk have been ripped open, stuffing spilling out, cigarette burns marr the once supple fabric. But he isn't looking at any of those things: he's looking at the metal folding chair sitting in the center of the room, he's looking at the unconscious man slumped in the seat, head hung low with an unbecoming mix of sweat and blood dripping from his brow.

He's looking at Derek.

Not so powerful now. He sizes up Derek's limp form hunched in the chair, his eyes darken, two black marbles, a fearful sight resting above his cruel scowl. He's almost done having to play nice. The charade is coming to an end, and how free he will feel to let his own anger take over. Sounds of teasing, laughter, and broken promises swarm in his mind almost too loud to bear. He gives a swift and hearty kick to the chair, and Derek falls to the floor, still bound to the metal leg. His head bounces once on the hardwood. His eyelids flutter, and a moan escapes his lips before he slips out of consciousness once more.

James bounces on his heels, ready to start the party. He doesn't bother setting Derek up; let him lie there, he thinks. The yearbooks that he watched Derek proudly flip through still sit in a heap in the corner where he threw them after hefting Derek into the room. *Derek should be proud of his investigation. He should show off his work.* On the floor by Derek's head, James neatly lays out the yearbooks, opening them to the marked pages. Derek can show off his findings when the gang's all here. The morning is rushing by, and he's got a party to host, so he slams the door to the den, locking Derek in, and grabs his keys and phone from the living room.

His pocket buzzes. *Two new messages.* He already knows what they will say, but he opens the most recent one anyway.

So annoying, but we're heading to Derek's early; want to pick me up?

"I sure do," he says out loud.

He fires off a quick response and opens the text he sent himself from Derek's phone an hour ago, arrogantly checking his handiwork. Glancing in the dusty cracked mirror on the wall, he ruffles his hair and cups a hand to check his breath. Grown-up James Myer gets his revenge with style. The floor creaks as he walks back to the mantel, giving one more look to the photo of the bright-eyed old lady and happy little boy. His finger grazes the wrinkled and faded edge. Blinking back tears, he smiles at the memory.

"Love you, Grandma."

34

"What does it say?" Jackson attempts to lean closer but his crutch wobbles, threatening to topple over.

"Um, it says; 'Guys, I know who it is. Meet me at the Doris house, dinner later.' Signed Derek." Whitney steps back, allowing Ellie and James to look at the hastily written note taped to the front door.

Ellie yanks it off the door, reading it over again. *Could he really have figured it out?*

"Who *it* is?" James looks to Ellie. "What's he talking about?" A perfect guise of confusion washes over his face.

Ellie lets out a sigh. "Long story, I'll fill you in on the way." She crumbles the note and shoves it into her pocket before stomping off down the porch.

"El, you sure that's a good idea?" Whitney wrinkles her brow.

"Might as well tell him, he's here."

"But—"

"Would you rather him just leave, and I ride with you guys? That's kind of rude, besides maybe he can help."

Whitney shoots Jackson a worried glance, but he shrugs, looking down at his leg. They both know he could use some extra help if needed. "That's fine. We'll meet ya'll over there."

Inward, James shivers with excitement. How funny that this is the time that they finally choose to include him.

Pulling her sweater tightly around her, Whitney lingers a moment. She watches as James throws an arm around Ellie, pulling her close, whispering in her ear as he opens the car door for her. She's not jealous, not exactly, but after all this time with Jackson under her roof, she can't understand why they aren't just honest with each other about their feelings. As much as she'd like to blame him, it's her that keeps holding back. What is it that keeps her from speaking up? There was a moment in the hospital, but ever since, it's like they just tip-toe around it, almost opening up but then closing themselves off when they get too close to actually talking it through, remaining stuck in the secrets of the house. It has to be obvious to him. She pulled away from him the other night, but there's such a long history. She needs to hear him say it. She stamps her feet in frustration; jealousy and shame are not things that she wants to think about today, not when she should be spending the morning with her mom and her daughter. As she walks back to her car, a whole new wave of regret washes over her. These past few weeks have forced so much time away from Melody. She wonders if this will be the Thanksgiving that Mel remembers the most when she's grown—the one her mother didn't spend with her.

The drive to the Doris house is awkward. He can sense the change in Whitney's mood, but there's nothing he can do to fix it. He could suggest she drop him off,---go back home to Mel, but he knows she wouldn't abandon him like that, and she's far too curious to know what Derek has uncovered. His hand reaches out for hers but stops short. She's driving, and right now, taking her by surprise isn't the best idea. He pulls his hand back to himself, wincing when his knees bang the glove box as she bumps over the train tracks.

They pull up shortly after James, and Whitney cuts the engine. "I don't see his Mustang."

"I don't know; maybe he parked somewhere else?" Jackson lets the question linger for a moment before shoving his door open and reaching for the crutches in the back.

"Here man; let me get those for you." James pulls the crutches out, leaning them against the car while he helps Jackson out of his seat.

"Thanks." Jackson nods.

"So…where is he?" Ellie asks, joining the group.

"I guess he could've parked in the garage." Jackson suggests.

"How would he have gotten in though? He could've left his car in his own garage and took a cab to get here, but that's weird." Ellie pulls at her hair, nervously twisting the ends before letting them fall and unravel.

"Maybe we should wait. It feels weird." Whitney backs up a few steps.

"His parents live out this way. He probably just walked over. I say we just go in and find out." Uncomfortable, Jackson leans heavily on his right crutch. It's quiet for a moment. Only the sounds of the cheerful chirps of nearby birds interrupt the hesitation.

"I don't know. Ellie filled me in. It sounds kind of dangerous." Playing it cool, James shrugs, concern all over his face.

"No, Jackson's right. We've got to check. If he's here, we can't just ditch him. I'll text him really quick, see if he responds." Whitney's fingers fly across her phone screen, the others watching, half expecting him to reply instantly.

"Well, if we're going, me and Jackson are going in first."

"I'm good with that." Jackson checks his balance, and hobbling on his crutches, follows James up the deteriorating steps.

Both shivering in the cold, Ellie and Whitney hover close together behind the guys, looking on as James shakes the doorknob.

"It's not locked." James steps through the doorway first, followed by Jackson and then Ellie. Whitney looks behind her through the bare trees to the road once more as a gust of wind whistles across her face, a whisper of a warning. With a heavy sigh, she follows her friends and crosses the dark threshold of the house.

"Hey man, can I see your phone for a sec? I left mine at my place." He's calm if not a little cocky. A sly grin barely grazes the corners of James's mouth in the darkness.

"Sure." Leaning to one side, Jackson fumbles in his pocket for a moment before unlocking and handing his phone over to James.

"It's just really dark in here." James hits the flashlight icon on the screen lighting the foyer. He's now got Derek and Jackson's phones; only two more to go.

"Derek!" Whitney shouts. "Derek, we're here."

"Derek, buddy! Are you here?" James calls out. It takes everything inside him to stifle a snicker because he knows it doesn't matter if Derek hears them or not. He can't respond—not only is his mouth gagged, but he was left unconscious. Who knows if he's awake yet.

"I don't like this." Ellie mumbles, backing into an overturned table. "Maybe we should just go."

"I don't know. I mean you know how he can be. He's probably cooked up some elaborate way to tell us whatever it is that he knows. We'll never hear the end of it if we abandon him on Thanksgiving," Jackson tries to reassure her.

"He would do that?" James asked, eyebrows raised.

"What? Concoct some crazy way of getting us all here to show off? Yeah, he would. He could've just texted us to come here instead of leaving some mysterious note on his door." Whitney rolls her eyes before checking her phone, no response. She's had enough of this. A dinner is one thing but to interrupt her morning and Thanksgiving lunch with her daughter is pretty unforgivable in her book. She's over this whole thing. Now, she just wants to find Derek, give him a piece of her mind, and dump the dinner to try to make it up to Melody. "Let's just find him and get out of here."

"I'm with you. We have families to see; this is just rude." Ellie can feel her new resolve sliding into annoyance.

"Okay, so what's the plan? Look for him together, split up? You guys want to check the back rooms?" James motions to Whitney and Jackson.

"No!" They both shout.

"I mean, it's not necessary; we should all look around together, and if he's not here, we leave," Jackson says firmly.

"Alright, so it looks like the living room and main

parts of the house are this way, but I'm not sure. I don't know the layout. I wasn't here either time that you guys came." *Here we go.*

"Either time?" Whitney's voice cracks. *What did Ellie tell him?*

"Well, yeah," he calls over his shoulder as he leads them toward the living room. "El told me you guys came when you were in college, which is apparently what this is all about. But, you guys came once before in high school, remember? I was supposed to come too, but then, I didn't. He stops and lowers his head, ready to see how they'll react to being called out.

Jackson stops in his tracks, crutches askew. "Oh. That's right. Man, I'm sorry about that. We were dumb kids. We probably forgot or something. We didn't even come inside the first time, none of us had the guts."

Not reading the room, Ellie smiles at the memory, a happy one for her – she was included. "Yeah, that was a good night. We just hopped the fence and lay out in the yard looking up at the stars through the trees. It was--"

"El." Whitney puts a hand on Ellie's shoulder, cutting her off with a quick shake of the head.

"Sounds nice," James says through his teeth.

The room grows awkwardly silent; Ellie sidles up to James weaving her arm through his. She can feel the muscles clinch through his sweater, but she hopes her carelessness doesn't run him off. The group makes their way to the kitchen, stopping to look around.

"Well, at least it's a little brighter in here, but what are those?" Whitney points to the two kitchen windows. "Why would you cover windows with blankets?"

"Painting? Maybe? Who knows. This place is so creepy," Jackson whispers in her ear.

"Well, I'm not seeing anything here. We should probably go back to the main room and branch out from there, yeah?" James shrugs his arm away from Ellie, leaving her with red-hot embarrassment coursing through her veins.

"Sure." She smiles though a warm blush creeps up her neck. Casually, she licks her lips and throws her head back to shake out her flowing hair, ready to make him rethink his choice. He'd have to be dead not to notice the way she looks from that angle.

It's her own fault, it's her own fault. The mantra plays on repeat until he can tear his eyes from her.

Together, they all huddle in the living room looking at the closed office door. Jackson notices the open alcove leading to the formal dining room just off to the side. The sight of it sends a shudder of fear so forceful down his body that his crutches wobble, momentarily throwing him off balance.

"What is this room?" Ellie's hand grazes the heavy wood of the door.

"I don't know. I never came in here," Whitney breathes.

Jackson turns to avoid seeing the dining room and takes in the space behind him, trying to convince himself to forget the leg and open the giant door that stands in front of him. But the light from his phone still in James's hand catches something on the mantle and he inches toward it. "Wait, look you guys. There's a photo up here."

The little boy and the old woman draw everyone in, and they stare at the two captured in time, seated on the steps of the house. Beyond that, they take in the discoloration and the creases and folds from the many years this picture has been around.

"Well, that's not creepy at all." Ellie laughs, sarcasm dripping from her mouth like honey.

"We're wasting time. Let's just find Derek and get the hell out of here." James moves to the door, impatiently waiting for the others to join him. With one hand gripping Jackson's phone, and the other wrapped around the knob, he throws his shoulder against the door, knocking it wide open, everyone tumbling inside.

"No, No!" Whitney trips over her feet, screams, and turns to race back through the door. But it slams closed. The others look back and see James, eyes black and arms crossed standing in front of the door, blocking the exit.

35

The crutches clatter to the floor, punctuating the silent horror that has filled the room since the last echo of Whitney's scream died out.

"Derek!" Jackson forgets all about his crutches as he limps as fast as he can to his unmoving friend. "Derek!" He yells again, shaking him violently. He notices the dark red running from Derek's matted head and stops the shaking, working quickly to pull the mottled strips of fabric from his mouth. That unmistakable metallic smell creeps into his nose, his mouth, choking him in the thick scent of his friend's blood.

"Is he alive?" Whitney cries.

"I don't know, I don't know." Jackson's throat begins to close, and he feels he may vomit any moment.

Ellie, pale-faced and trembling, moves closer. "What is that in front of him?"

"Maybe that's the evidence he's been searching for," James responds.

All three of them turn to stare at James, not comprehending why he is still standing by the door and not moving to help them with Derek.

The thrill of watching them all so completely overcome with horror fills James with the satisfaction he craves. He pockets Jackson's phone and creeps closer to the group.

"They're yearbooks," Whitney says to no one. "I

think they're his."

Derek lies motionless as the three lean in, recognizing the picture of themselves during field day. It quickly dawns on each of them that James is standing in the background watching them, in the photo and in reality. Ellie quickly grabs the other yearbook, a strangled cry bursting from deep inside her. She thrusts the book at Jackson as she collapses beside Derek in a fit of sobs. Right away, he notices that he's looking at James's senior page. "It's the same photo," his voice shakes. He looks at Whitney, understanding and terror in his eyes. "It's the same photo as the one on the mantle. The old lady and the little boy."

"This is not happening, this is not happening, this is not happening…" she whispers it over and over under her breath as she scrambles to pull her phone from her purse. As fast as she can, she unlocks the screen, her hands shaking uncontrollably. "Shit!" She screams as she loses grip and the phone slides from her hands, landing on the floor with a loud crack. She whirls around to grab it, but James gets to it first.

"I'll just hold on to that," he says, with a slow wink.

Focused on James's movements, Ellie discreetly reaches into her back pocket, pulling out her own phone. She's frightened, but Derek lying helpless next to her motivates her to try. She moves her shoulder letting her hair fall into a black curtain around her, and she turns on her phone. She cringes as the screen lights up the dark room, kicking herself for always keeping her screen so bright. Slowly, she takes her eyes off James for a moment, looking down to pull up the keypad, but he's too quick. He gets to her in seconds. She tries to back up but bumps into Derek, letting out a scream and throwing her phone at James as he thrusts his once charismatic face directly in front of her.

"Oh, Ellie," he teases. "I thought you out of everyone would put up the most fight." With the tips of his fingers, he strokes her cheek and she recoils, repulsed at the very thought of having ever allowed him to touch her. "That's disappointing."

Through her tears, she manages to sputter out; "It's you in the photo. Why are you doing this?"

"Yes! There she goes, folks. Come on El, get mad; you know you want to. Show me that fury, that anger that you love! Why don't you hit me? Or would you rather have a baseball bat? Or perhaps, a can of spray paint?"

He knows. Of course, he knows about Minneapolis. He'd have to in order to mess with her resume, but he knows everything. He knows more than the fact that she went into the house that night; he knows what she did here too. It's in his eyes.

"Baseball bat? Spray paint? Ellie, what is he talking about?" Whitney cries.

Ellie's phone now firmly clenched in his hand, James stands. "You don't know? Well, we will save that bit for later. It'll make excellent dinner conversation, my friends. Unless of course, the two of you want to sneak off to a bedroom. Yeah?" Using the phone, he motions to Jackson and Whitney. His smirk is callous and frightening, and it makes Whitney feel exposed, like he can see right through her.

"James!" Jackson yells. He tries to stand up, but James promptly turns, kicking the boot out from under him. Jackson's back hits the floor with a sickening thump. Tears and sobs mix in a guttural scream from deep within Whitney.

From the floor, Derek stirs; his head throbs, and he can feel the effects of the drugs and the attack, but his mind is unclear on what exactly happened and what's going on until his eyes focus, and he spots a pair of brown dress shoes. He struggles to tilt his head back and look up– James. In a whirlwind of pain and anger, it all comes rushing back to him. Waking up feeling hungover and out of it again, spotting the bare dresser where the yearbooks were supposed to be, running into the living room and being hit over the head, struggling to pull away as he went in and out of consciousness, getting a glimpse of James as he was thrown into the car, before it all went black again, and now, waking up here. On the floor. Watching James stand between all of his friends. *Oh, my God.* He was too late; James figured out what he knew.

"Derek!" Ellie notices his open eyes and slides to him, throwing her arms around him and pulling him into an awkward, messy hug. She's not sure if she's comforting herself or him, but either way, she buries her face in his neck and cries, her whole body shakes with the force of her tears.

Everyone watches the two of them. For a moment, nobody moves except for the trembling of Ellie's shoulders as she holds onto Derek like a lifeline. He was right not to trust James; she should've known.

"Derek! You're up! So sorry we had a change of venue, you understand I'm sure."

At the sound of his name, Derek pushes Ellie aside, looking at the same hollow, humorless face of the man that brought him here. He should've told everyone it was James from the moment he suspected it, but he knows deep down they never would have believed him. It had to come to this.

"I thought this party was better suited for *my* house. We'll all have a nice long chat over dinner in a little while. Happy Thanksgiving!" Glancing at his watch, James clasps his hands together with excitement. "Well, look at the time! I've got to get our dinner going! I'll take you guys to your rooms in just a second." He walks to the back of the room to the built-in cabinets behind the large desk. One cabinet door at the top is open and unbroken. He tosses Ellie's phone inside and pulls the other phones from his front pockets, throwing them in as well. The cabinet door slams shut and he grabs a small silver key from the desktop, locking the cabinet before calmly returning to the stunned group.

An uncomfortable hush falls over the space; no one wants to catch the attention of James, but it's unavoidable, he's looking around the room making sure to meet the eye of each person, trapping them into his world.

Finally, Ellie glances up, more timid than ever before. "Our rooms?"

"Of course. I would never turn you out after a long night of celebrating! Besides, you guys came here before wanting a good scare right? So, let's get started!"

Whitney turns, sizing up the distance to the door, but before she can force her legs to move, James begins to laugh.

"Oh, sweetheart," He drawls. "I wouldn't do that." Casually, he pulls a long knife from the sheath hidden in the back of his jeans. Jackson's head snaps back as James leans forward, grabbing him by his hair, all the while staring at Whitney's horrified face.

"I wasn't—I won't!" She stutters.

"Good answer." He pulls Jackson off the floor and roughly shoves him toward Whitney. "It's time to show you all to your rooms."

36

Warped and dusty, peeling, brown wallpaper hangs in awkward strips barely clinging to the wall. That same wallpaper that haunts Whitney's dreams, the same wallpaper that crinkled under Jackson's hand as he leaned toward Whitney, pushing against it. They're in the back bedroom, Jackson and Whitney. Just as they were nine years ago, only this time, they don't want to be here. Each bound by thick rope to a metal folding chair, side by side in the middle of the room. It's dark, but James has at least left them a battery powered lamp on the floor close to the door.

Frustrated, Jackson looks around, taking in the dated and dismal surroundings. He didn't bother really seeing this room the last time he was here; it had been dark and he was far too focused on her. His heart aches as she quietly sobs beside him although she attempts to hold it together. Tortured by her cries, his head falls to his chest. A soft buzz whips by his left ear, a fly. He can't swat it away, so he doesn't bother to try. It flies back and forth, teasing. A little tickle by his ear, a little tickle at his neck.

This is my fault. If I didn't have this stupid boot on my foot, I could've gotten us out of this.

He wants to say something, anything, to make it better, but the right words just won't come. There isn't anything he can say to fix this situation. They walked right into James's trap.

So, he stares at the strips and scraps of that moldy,

old paper and wonders where James has taken Derek and Ellie, and if they're okay. He and Whitney have only been in this room for maybe a half an hour, but not knowing what's going on in the rest of the house is driving him crazy. He's terrified of what James may do to Ellie, but how did she not see what was coming? *How did I not see it?* It's too quiet; he strains his ears to listen, but he can't hear anything. They've been put in the last bedroom, so it's far away, but he should still be able to hear loud noises if there are any.

It begins to dawn on him, the answer to Whitney's question in the kitchen. The thick blankets hanging in every room, they're not there just because. They are there to block out sound. Screams, maybe. What is James planning on doing? His pulse quickens, and a barrage of awful, horrifying scenarios flash in his mind. His neck tingles, he can't catch his breath, and he realizes that he is panicking. He has to think about something else, anything else.

"Whit! Are you hurt?" he whispers.

Looking up at him through tear-soaked lashes, she whispers back, "No, are you?"

"I'm okay." He wants to ask her so much, what she thinks they should do, where the others may be, but he doesn't want to upset her worse than she already is. Anyway, she won't have answers anymore than he does. Maybe he can reassure her, tell her he will get her out of here safely to her daughter. But, bringing up Melody would cause more damage. And what if he can't keep that promise?

Silently, they sit, helpless and staring at that wall. Their old memory will forever be tainted by this moment if they make it out. Excitement replaced with fear. The tears roll down Whitney's face. Her eyes burn and her nose is wet, but her hands are painfully tied behind her back, and there isn't anything she can do to clean herself up.

"Why is he doing this?" she asks.

"I have no idea. But it seems pretty clear the old lady in the photo with him was his grandma, and I would guess that this was her house, and that her name was Doris." He lowers his voice. James could be anywhere, lurking, listening.

"I get that, but why us? There were tons of kids that

broke in after she died, tons of kids that spread stories about her when she was alive for that matter. We didn't know they were related. We didn't start the rumors; we were just four of many that came here. I had no idea he was even connected to this place," she whispers back.

"I don't know his reasons. Whatever it is that we did, or he thinks we did--this is obviously not a normal reaction to…anything." Straining his neck, he turns his head as far as he can to assess the room.

Maybe there's something here we can use.

A large and dusty four-poster bed frame rests behind them, covered in cobwebs and scratches. The broken mattress sags inside of it, not a trace of any comfort. Yellowed and soiled sheets adorn the top. A relic, a room lost in time. Two rusted, silver springs protrude through the side of the mattress fabric, drawing him in for a moment, but sadly, he knows it'll be of no use to get them out of here.

37

"I'm sorry, I'm so sorry. I should've listened." Huddled on the floor next to Derek, Ellie intertwines her arms with his. She can see that he is in a lot of pain, but she's frozen with fear. There's not much more she can do for him other than to hold him and whisper her apologies over and over. Once again, Derek was right, and she seems to have gotten them into their biggest mess yet.

The office door flies open, and she slinks back into Derek. He puts a hand protectively over her shoulder.

"Ellie! It's time for you to get some rest before dinner, darlin'. I have a special room just for you."

Flinching; she can't hold her ground as he roughly pulls her from her tangle-hold with Derek. "Don't worry, you'll see him again soon." He drags her to the door, but just before shoving her through, she turns for a moment, locking eyes with Derek. If only she could send him a message through her stare, but he nods back anyway, knowing that even though he is badly beaten, she's the one who needs reassurance.

It's no use to dig her heels in; he pulls her toward the hallway and into the first room on the right. With much of his force, he hurls her onto the bed, grabbing both of her arms and locking them together on the bedpost with handcuffs.

"I know you're far more familiar with the dining room, but you'll just have to make do here. With these cuffs you won't be able to break anything or graffiti anything either."

Her soft, doe eyes widen from the implication. Tears gather in her eyelids threatening to spill down her cheeks. Her arms are twisted, made painfully immobile by the cuffs.

"Now, don't get upset. We really could have been something if things were different. You are hard to give up; I'll give you that." He puts his hand to her cheek, stroking the skin, but her body won't let her hide her disgust. She twists her legs on the mattress, sliding back on the bed as much as she can. His hand connects with her mouth in a hard slap that has the tears flowing freely now. She coughs, choking on her sobs. "But you're not different; that's the problem with you Ellie," he sings. "You're the same as you've always been."

"What do you want from me?" she whispers.

Ignoring her, he stands and walks to the dresser, grabbing an old wooden photo frame resting on top. He carries it back to her side and places it on the nightstand. The shiny hard glass is just out of her reach.

"This is Doris and Wade, my grandparents. Now, they were quite the couple." The bed shifts under his weight as James sits beside Ellie. "My grandmother—she saw the good in everyone, or at least she tried to. That's just how she was. But I saw the sadness she felt after my grandpa died, all those rumors about her. She was old; this house was old. All those kids knocking on her door and screaming right in her face. She didn't deserve that. And she didn't deserve me hiding out in the backyard every time I came to visit, just so no one would know that I knew her. She didn't deserve to be hurt like that, hurt by her own grandchild, the way that you all made me hurt her."

"I never came here as a kid," Ellie mumbles.

"No, you didn't. You came when you should've been old enough to know better. You came and you had no problems destroying her house, her memories. Tell me, did it make you feel better?"

"No."

"So, it was all for nothing," he laughs. "Of course. It's never deeper with you. Well, we can talk more later. There's a lot to discuss over dinner tonight. Why don't you get some rest?"

James eases himself off the bed and walks to the door.

"Wait—" She whispers.

James stops, turning to look at Ellie and gives her a smile before walking through the door and locking her in from the outside.

"No, no no no no!" She wails. Tugging and twisting, she pulls hard on the handcuffs, but they are solid and tight. Red marks form on her wrists proving as much. The wood and glass photo frame on the nightstand sits just out of reach, mocking her. She could try to kick it closer, or slide it with her feet, but she can't twist that way. It'll never work. She dissolves into deep, painful sobs, her chest heaving as she struggles to catch her breath. Panic takes over.

What have I done?

Thinking back over their quick but intense relationship, she searches her memory to find any clue she may have overlooked. There had to have been signs that were missed. He's hated her all this time. Was he really that good at faking, or was she so self-involved as to miss every red flag thrown her way? Probably a little of both.

Her heart knocks in her chest; it beats so fast she worries it could burst from her body. Her head spins; how are her friends doing? Are they okay; are they alive? Overwhelmed by the thought of losing them and being trapped, this room she's locked in with its solid, dark dresser, and old sewing table, swirls as her vision tunnels and her world shrinks until she's slumped on the bed, head hanging down, arms bound tightly above her.

38

The waiting is the worst part. Time seems to tick by and stand still all at once. Derek is sure that James will be back to kill him any moment. Was he joking when he mentioned dinner, or will there really be another chance to get out of this? Because if he isn't dead, that's what it will be. An opportunity. The chair he was in lies on its side just behind him; he scoots back as much as his injured limbs allow and rests his back on the hard metal of the chair legs.

I should've figured it out sooner. If they only would've listened when I told them I didn't like him.

His anger ignites.

I told her to stay away from him. How many times do they have to screw up before they listen?

The veins in his neck pop out, fury flashing through him like some sort of super power. It's their fault he's here, beaten and locked in a room. It's their fault if he dies.

His mind takes off, thoughts racing through his head, ideas fighting each other to come to the surface. There has to be a way to save himself, and he means himself. Only himself. If they don't want to listen to him, then there's no reason he should continue on playing their hero. The yearbooks left in a heap taunt him, one splayed open to the photo of him and his friends. Maybe there is one reason. Maybe if he had never backed off, never given up his need to control, he could've prevented this. They should know that his judgment is far superior.

Quickly, he begins to form a plan. It's perfect, really. Just like nine years ago when he was almost their savior that night. But time and chance have given him another opportunity, and this time he won't let it slip away. He just has to find his way in. This time the stakes are even better.

The door is flung open. Footsteps land hard on the wood floor as James makes his way toward Derek. "Derek!" He loudly sings out. "It's your turn. But you don't need to go anywhere, do you? Because you were here in this room that night, yeah?"

"Look psycho, I have no idea what you're talking about." It's a risk, responding this way, but Derek decides the only way to get inside of James's head is to antagonize him. Anger him, then break him.

James stalks closer. His foot comes down hard on Derek's hand; bones or knuckles pop loudly, and he leans down, breathing directly into his face. "I don't know who you think you're talking to, but this is my house now. I was here that night. I saw what you were doing. I saw you with those matches in your hand. You have no idea how lucky you were that the cop came when he did."

"You don't know anything!" Derek spits.

"I know your plan didn't work. Your friends left you anyway. You would sacrifice *my* house for those idiots!"

Derek forces himself to not be shaken. "They're back now, aren't they? We're all in this together, aren't we?" He screams, flailing his free hand out in the air.

"Who do you think made that happen? I brought you all together. I did this. They wouldn't be here without me." James slaps a hand to his chest, proud of his work. "You think your little coffee shop meetings made you closer; you would've had nothing to meet about if it weren't for the things I've done. This has been a long time coming."

Making him angry worked for a while, but Derek senses James will leave the room soon if he doesn't keep him talking. He's already backing up, so Derek pulls his crushed hand to him, nursing his injury and changing his tactic. "Okay, you got me there. But how could you have known Ellie was coming back? None of us knew until Whitney ran into her." If Derek has learned anything in his lifetime of initiating outcomes, it's that stroking an ego will almost always get you the information you want.

Satisfied with being able to one up Derek, James leans back on his heels, hands in his pockets. "When you're the gawky kid, the one the other kids run away from, pick last, you tend to develop hobbies, lots of hobbies to fill the time. But, you see, people on the internet don't know you. There are people out there just like you, who feel the same way, and they can teach you things. I learned a lot about hacking. I've never been one to let a good grudge die, although now…" he chuckles. "I've checked in from time to time. I saw it in her emails."

Horrified, Derek quickly twists the disgust on his face to a look of fascination. "You've been watching us all these years?"

"Oh, yeah. You're not who you used to be, you know. In fact, I'd say you might be the very one who has changed the most."

"What do you mean?" Derek asks.

"Oh, come on! Derek Steven!" he booms. "The kid who could be friends with anybody, the one people listened to, the one with all the influence. Mr. Popular! You could convince anyone of anything. I always saw it. You had such power over everyone around you; it's why I always asked *you* if you and your friends wanted to hang out. If you said yes, they would too. You used to be a leader. But now, you're just a sad shell of yourself; they all hate you; you know."

They don't really hate me, do they? They came here and found me; there's no way.

"If they hate me so much, why did they come here today?"

"Oh, buddy, they aren't here to save you. Everyone is here because of a note I left from you. Telling them that you were here and knew who was behind everything. They just wanted the games to stop, that's all."

Here it is, my chance. Derek steadies his breathing. "And they trusted that I could be the one to stop it. They always turn to me. They always will. That's what you want, isn't it? I mean, sure you've got to avenge your grandmother's house and good name; we nearly destroyed the place. And we ditched you in high school, barely gave you a thought. You want that power; you crave it. You had a little taste of it dating Ellie, and you want more. It takes more than just switching up your look. I can help you. I can help you get them on your side or get rid of them. Whatever you want, but either way, you win."

James kneels down on the floor next to Derek. Cautiously, he feels for the knife in his back pocket. "And what do you get out of that?"

"My life. That's it. I walk away and you get all the attention, all the glory. Me? I'm gone; I don't want it anymore. It's all yours."

Rubbing his forehead, James takes a moment to consider what that would be like before backing away from Derek. He jerks the knife from his pocket, pointing it at Derek. "No. No way. Even you can't get them on my side now. They're all tied up. They won't just get over that."

So they're still alive.

"I can. But like I said, you want them on your side, or you want them gone. Either way, I can do it."

"What if I want them on my side but still want them to pay a little?"

"Let me handle it. Put the knife down. You kill me, and then how do you do this? How do you spin things? Because trust me, we *can* spin this. It's not too late."

James closes his eyes, taking deep, calming breaths. His hand shakes slightly as he puts the knife away. His confidence shaken, he tries to mask it. "What's your plan?"

"You're hosting dinner tonight, right? We'll start there."

39

Four white pillar candles flicker in the dark dining room, trails of wax slide down the sides. Evening is rolling in, but because of the thick sheets hanging from the window pane, no one will be able to notice.

James stands back, examining his grandparents' antique table. He's placed a cold turkey-substance frozen meal in front of each of the five crumbling chairs. Not bothering to remove any of the dust or broken fragments from the table, he throws down a plastic fork beside each un-microwaved dish. Let them eat with the mouse droppings and jagged glass; let them be as uncomfortable as he has always been.

He fills five paper cups from an old bottle of water, only a dash for his friends, and pours the most for himself. *I deserve it after all the hard work of preparing this dinner party.*

Unfortunately, the room is open with a large alcove built into the side wall, so he won't be able to lock any doors. He moves on to the business of loping a thick rope to the spindles of the chairs. He'll just have to tie them down; it's the only option.

The knife rests in its sheath in his back pocket, just tingling with the need to be used. This is the only shot he's allowing Derek; if he does his job, James will go through with the deal they've ironed out. And if he doesn't do his job, the knife will get its chance.

After fastening the final rope, he shuffles from the

room to get Derek. Leaning down with a hand on the knife handle, he looks Derek in the eye. "One wrong move is all it takes. You die, they die. Got it?"

"You have my word."

James grabs the knife, holding it to Derek's back as they make their way down the hall toward their first stop. He waits by the door as Derek quickly uncuffs Ellie from the bed. Sniffling beside Derek, Ellie trips over her own shoes, desperately trying to blow the hair out of her face through her tears. *Not so lovely now.* With something akin to pride, James watches on as Derek roughly pulls her along. Once in the dining room, he shoves her down into a chair as James makes quick work of tying her to it and releasing her hands, so that she can at least eat. After all, he's not a monster.

He stands, twisting his hands together, excited. "Alright, just two more to go. Derek?"

"You got it." Derek tosses the handcuff keys back to James and together they slink back out of the room.

Her pale green eyes, now reddened and lackluster, flick back and forth from the men. She thought she'd been saved—Derek walking into her lonely room by himself with the small set of keys. She felt buoyed with hope. She could taste the freedom and was so sure he was there to rescue her. Her legs had twitched—primed to run. Then she saw *him* waiting for her just outside the door.

"I'm sorry Ellie. I have to. I'll get us out of this somehow, but for now, I have to do this." Derek had whispered as he leaned over her.

She'd asked why, and he hadn't answered. He just slipped the key in the lock and released her arms from the bedpost, twisting them to the front of her and snapping the cuffs on, once again prohibiting her movement. He paid no attention to the tears streaming down her face. Her body had felt so heavy. It didn't want to cooperate, but she couldn't let it take over. Not with her hands cuffed together and Derek's firm grip on her upper arm. He walked her down to the dining room with James leering at her as they moved. She caught a small wink from Derek just as they entered the disgusting space. She wonders if she can trust it. Shouldn't he have freed her and tried to help her run? Why help James, especially since he hates him? She can't bear the thought that they may have cooked this whole thing up together. But Derek's blood on the floor of that office was real. She feels the cold gaze of James on her as they push Whitney and Jackson into the room. The pair tied together, each by an arm.

Their entrance is loud, clunky; Jackson hasn't been given his crutch, and with Derek pulling him along by his one free arm, he has nowhere to lean. Forced to put his full weight down on his boot, his face betrays the pain with every unsynchronized step they take. They're thrust into two chairs, side by side at the table. The chairs are just a hair too far apart to be comfortable and Whitney nearly slips off of her seat. James takes over for Derek, tying them by their bellies to the chair. Stepping back, he rubs his chin, satisfied with the way things are working out and satisfied with Derek's cooperation.

"Derek, you can take a seat now."

The others eye Derek suspiciously as he sits, obedient. The looks are not missed by James, and he hesitates for a second before taking the last rope and tying Derek to his chair. Best to play it safe. He makes his way to the old hearth, leaning against the brick mantle. Standing there amongst the debris and graffiti and trash, he gazes at his guests before taking a big swig of his water and placing the cup on the mantel. The king of his own haunted house.

"Good evening everyone, and Happy Thanksgiving! Welcome to my home. I'm so pleased that you all could join me. It's going to be quite a special night. We have a lot to discuss, but I'll let you all have your dinner first. After all, it's a holiday!" Grabbing his cup, he takes his seat at the head of the table and thrusts his drink high into the air. "To friendship!"

No one dares to move. "Just like old times I see; me going out of my way to please you all, and you making absolutely no effort!" The weak paper cup folds a little at the bottom from the force of the slam. "My new girlfriend doesn't even want to raise a glass in celebration?" He pulls the knife from its sheath and sets it next to his meal, keeping it close and in sight. He wants them to see it.

The blood drains from her face. Her hair hangs limp and tangled, and mascara stains mar her perfect skin as Ellie tries to control the shaking of her hand while she clenches the cup. "Cheers," she forces from gritted teeth.

"That's better. Let's eat!" Plunging the plastic fork into the thin slice of cold, congealed meat, he's aware that all eyes are focused on him. He loves this feeling, being the center of their attention. It's more powerful than watching from a window. He shoves a forkful into his mouth, grinning as he chews. Whitney stares, pale-faced as if she may throw up. The meal includes a gluey helping of mashed potatoes and gravy and James eagerly dives into it as well.

"What's the matter?" He asks. "Why are none of you eating? Surely, you'd all be eating and laughing had you been at Derek's today."

"Come on James, this is disgusting. Just tell us what you want." Jackson speaks for the first time since entering.

A hush falls over the room; the only sound comes from an empty stomach growling. After a long, uncomfortable moment, James stands. The air around him is charged with electricity; anger fuels him. "I'm sorry? Is my Thanksgiving meal disgusting to you? I'd love to know what's wrong with it. Derek, will you please relieve Jackson of his plate?"

Jackson stares straight ahead as Derek reaches across the table to scoop up the plastic t.v. dinner tray. He slides it through the muck on the table toward James.

Picking up the plate of food, James smiles. "It's okay, Jackson. You don't have to eat it all, but please, just have a taste." He hurls the dinner across the table so violently that it smacks Jackson in the face, a bit of soggy mashed potatoes splashes into Whitney's eye. "Didn't your mother teach you not to insult your host's cooking?"

A rogue laugh sits in the back of Derek's throat; desperately, he tries to shove it down. Any other time, Jackson's face covered with food would be hilarious, but under these circumstances... he has to play it cool, has to walk the thin line between proving himself to James, and getting his friends to trust him. That familiar feeling comes creeping back up, attaching itself to his thoughts. Excitement tingles all the way down his spine. It's that need. He may have had to take a beating, but no one could deny that this is his ultimate test. He may have failed to get them on his side about James before, but he was holding back. All of these years of self-restraint have come to an end. They got themselves into this, and James has had his fun, but it's his turn now. It's Derek's turn to control the outcome. Manipulation. It's an art form, really. And no one weaves a better tapestry. If he lets it out—and he will, he won't likely ever reign it back in. It's his show now.

40

"What the hell, James?" Ellie screams automatically. Her eyes widen, horrified that the words came out of her mouth, afraid of what the monster in front of her may do.

"Oh, Ellie. What's a little bit of thrown food in the middle of a room that you yourself destroyed?" He waves his arms, motioning to the curio, the shattered glass, the spray paint.

"You did this?" Whitney whispers, turning her head to Ellie.

Ellie's stare hardens at the memory; that night she was broken, she needed her friends. They didn't need her though, they had other ideas. Slowly, she nods.

"But, why?"

"Why? I needed you guys." She stares straight at Jackson, at the wet sludge dripping off of his face. "I was upset. I was on the verge of getting kicked out of school. I found Blake with some girl. I-it was just too much. I wanted to be with my friends. I needed someone to talk to and I just wanted encouragement. You two only wanted each other, and I was angry. I had to let it out somehow. You weren't there when I needed you. None of you."

"We didn't know." Jackson hangs his head.

"No, you didn't. You guys were busy running off to the back room together, and you think no one noticed, but *I* did. I saw the looks on your faces when we left. I saw your ruffled hair, your wrinkled clothes."

"I saw you, too." James winks at Whitney across the table. Repulsed; chills explode over her body.

"How do you even know any of this; you weren't here!" Jackson shouts at James.

"Oh but Jackson, I was. You people seem to keep forgetting that we didn't just go to high school together. We went to the same college as well. You just kept on pretending that I didn't exist. I saw you three." His finger moves from Jackson to Whitney to Derek. "You were outside of the dining room on campus. I was at a table nearby, and I heard you. Derek, the ring-leader planning a little ghost hunting trip. Out of desperation, it seemed. I never forgot how you invited me along that very first time, only to ditch me. But I thought maybe they've changed. I'll give them another chance. All I wanted was your friendship, but you guys couldn't let anyone else in. You remember, don't you? I walked up to your table to say hi. I asked what you guys were doing later, and do you remember what you said?"

"Oh my God! What does it even matter? We didn't want to hang out with you! No one was obligated to be your friend. *Maybe* you should've checked your weird obsession." Exasperated, Ellie lashes out.

He pauses, not bothering to respond to her outburst before continuing his story. "Derek shrugged his shoulders, and sweet little Whitney, you lied to me. You mumbled something about writing a paper before you got up and scurried away. But I came anyway. What does it feel like to realize that I was inside with you the whole time, and none of you knew?" He laughs loudly, picking up the knife and twisting it around in his hand. "I even managed to sneak into this room to leave Ellie a little present under the table while she was having her meltdown. She didn't find it, but someone else did. Right, Jack?"

"Oh, my God," Jackson breathes. "It wasn't real."

"Something like that will stick with you for years, huh?" His gaze moves to Whitney, who sits wild eyed and stiff with fear. His shoulders dance, so proud of himself. "I grabbed an old mannequin from my grandma's sewing closet, ripped the leg off, and left it to scare Ellie into stopping her madness. You came to destroy my grandparents house and blow me off at the same time? No. I was making sure that wouldn't happen again. Ellie never saw it, but Jackson did. You can't imagine the sheer terror in his eyes as he spotted it on his way out. It was incredible!"

"You never told me that." Whitney reaches for Jackson's hand, but the rope tightens into her stomach with the effort. She's not close enough.

Done holding his tongue; Derek slaps the table, sending dust motes floating in the candle light. "So, the whole time you guys were hooking up while Ellie was playing a one woman demolition derby? We could've figured this whole thing out if ya'll would've told me what the hell you were doing. It's because of you we're here right now." Fully aware of his own hypocrisy, the need for control outweighs the guilt.

"Right, and you're such a saint. We still don't know what you were doing that night? The whole thing was your idea in the first place," Ellie spits.

"It was my idea to hang out, not to tear the house apart." He lies. "I just walked around, looking through the rooms, what I assumed you guys were doing."

"Sure. Well, now's your chance to expose him. If you know where we all were, where was he?" Ellie turns to face James still not being able to wrap her mind around the man full of hatred in front of her being the same man that held her hand and carried her groceries. She actually let him meet her parents. It dawns on her that she may have seen them for the last time this morning.

Looking out at his guests, James pauses, thinking. Derek has done what he's been asked so far; he'll need this chance if he is to continue their deal. "I never saw him."

41

In his younger days, Derek used to love to challenge himself—a game to keep him on his toes. What a high he felt after telling a girl that she looked nice in a certain color, just to see her wear that very color day after day. Or when he caused a rivalry between friends by telling his teammate Kevin, that he was the best player on their basketball team, but he should watch out for Jason because he's been practicing all hours of the night and is getting better. That high was something, but it wasn't anything compared to the power he feels watching the man who clearly wanted to kill him, planned to kill him, stand there and lie for him right now. Everything else was just practice. If he can get control over this situation, there isn't anything he can't do.

There's just one piece of the puzzle missing, and with one question, he knows he'll have James under his thumb.

"Like I said, I was just exploring the house. Not defiling it. But that's not what really matters is it? I want to know why you tried to buy the place." Derek levels his gaze, challenging Jackson.

"What?" Jackson slides his arm across his face, slinging a glob of food off onto the floor.

"You might as well tell the truth. We all know. I saw the papers in your office," Ellie says.

Whitney says nothing, just holds her face in her hands. Too many revelations have come to light. And this weird thing between Derek and James when they hated each other days ago. Nothing is what it seemed before, and she's not sure she wants to hear what comes next. What if Jackson's answer changes everything? Are any of these people someone that she can trust?

Jackson sniffs, composing himself. "I swear it's not anything that you think. It's stupid, really. I don't even know why I put an offer on it. It's hard to explain, but James was right about the leg thing. I saw it when we were leaving; the house was more than creepy—I was terrified. The cops were coming, and it looked so real. I thought maybe I didn't really see it, then later on, what if it was real and something awful happened to someone and I didn't report it. He was right. It stayed with me for all these years. I have no idea what I was thinking, I could've asked for a tour and checked to see if it was here although I guess it wouldn't have been, but when I saw the listing, I don't know..." He leans his head back, exhaling deeply before speaking again. "It was a way to set things right, maybe? If there was really someone's leg, the realtor would've found it and reported it, and if not, I thought I could clear out the bad memories, fix it up, make it into a place where we could come together to make new memories. It felt like the only way for me to let the bad go. It sounds crazy, but I thought maybe the place that tore us apart could bring us back together. After all, not all of my memories here were bad." He gives Whitney a wan smile, longing for the time when their lives weren't so serious, so dangerous. "I realized what a ridiculous idea it was after the offer was rejected. And then Ellie came back and all this stuff started happening to you guys and I told you I didn't believe it because I just wanted to stop thinking about it. I thought maybe I caused all of it by trying to buy the house. If I pretended everything was a coincidence, then I could block it out."

"And then you fell." Whitney looks up.

"It was his turn." James laughs.

"I'm so sorry. I should've told you guys; I just didn't know how."

That slight, that one little slight of them ignoring what he just said wriggles its way into James's mind. Brushing past his joke, because even here, it's all about them. The feeling is shifting—it's quickly turning into a group therapy session. and once again, he isn't included. *They should be scared; they should be apologizing to me, begging me to keep them alive!*

It enrages him to watch them seated around *his* table, trapped by *him*, and yet still only be concerned about themselves and their relationships. His eyes narrow, and his body trembles as he loses his composure. He has to get control back. There's no time to wait on whatever plan Derek has.

"Enough!" He screams, hurling the knife forward with no regard for its direction. His vision wavers as the knife flies. It all blurs into red. Their screams bring him back, finally, they're no longer acting as though this is a bonding retreat. They're afraid of him; they respect him. As his sight clears, he sees the horrified faces of the group he so badly wanted to be a part of. He no longer wants that; he just wants them gone. In a way, he knew that's where it would land— the knife. He didn't need to see to throw it right into Ellie's chest.

Blood pours from the wound, and she sputters, slouching in her chair.

"What did you do?" James cries as tears spill down his face.

With everyone tied to their seats by their stomachs, no one is able to try to stop the bleeding. Ellie whimpers, and the weight of what he has done crashes down over James. Doubt creeps in. Though he's thought about it many times, he's never actually stabbed anyone before.

"It's your own fault; it's your own fault," He whispers it over and over.

Placing the blame at her feet has become his new mantra. He loved the cat and mouse game. He even loved stalking them, terrorizing them, but this feels different, not like he thought it would. He can't look at her.

He pulls the knots from Derek's chair and walks away. "Derek," he struggles to steady his voice. "There's an old wine cellar downstairs from the kitchen; please take her there for now."

He's a planner; he's meticulously planned every detail of their punishments, of their downfall, and of their kidnapping, but he never planned how this would end, and now it seems there's only one option. Somewhere deep down, he knew the outcome, but had he thought about it he might have lost his nerve. They're not getting out of this house, he won't let them.

Everyone watches as Derek fumbles with the rope, finally pulling it apart and releasing Ellie. He hoists her into his arms, not sure whether she is alive or not, and carries her out of the room, blood dripping onto his clothes as he leaves.

Turning his back to his last two hostages, James faces the hearth, his wheels spinning, trying to form a plan.

"James," Whitney says quietly, cautiously. "We can help you. You can let us go. There's time; you can still let us go. We'll all go together. We'll just say we were over at Derek's, and she never showed up."

"No, no, no, no. I picked her up at her parents' house. This is the end of it. It's what I was supposed to do."

"It's not! It was an accident, right? We can say that you brought her to Derek's, got into an argument, and she left. We don't know how she got here; it could work!" Desperation fills her voice. She'll say anything for this to be over, and Ellie needs help. Time is running out. "This can work. Go get Derek; we'll do just what I said."

James turns on his heel, his face illuminated eerily in the candlelight. His features appear to have morphed, and she can't see how she didn't notice the evil in them until today. The time for denying himself is over. He's ready to step into life as he really is, as he was meant to be. A loner, a killer. The keeper of the haunted house.

"None of you seem to know what the word "enough" means, so let me explain. It means stop talking. Stop doing anything, just stop!" He screams, freeing himself from every last emotion, and with a force he never knew he had, he flings their ropes from the chairs and grabs them both, dragging them down the hallway to what has become their room. Jackson slips on his boot, infuriating James. James shoves him across the room into the dresser. His face hits the top drawer and he slides to the ground, swollen and unable to move. His blood pools on the floor around him.

James's hand is so tightly wrapped around Whitney's wrist that her arm is turning blue, and he whips her around, shoving her back up against the wall. Her head slams against it, and as she falls, wisps of brown wallpaper float down around her. Maybe she loved Jackson, here, surrounded by the wallpaper, and maybe she'll die with Jackson, with the wallpaper, here. A piece lands in her hair, but she doesn't notice. She can't keep her eyes open. Brown paper scraps rain down on her like dirty snowflakes as she collapses.

42

Thick, warm blood trails down the front of Derek's pant leg, dripping onto the floor of the dank cellar. Ellie's bleeding steadily, but it'll be a lot worse if that knife comes out. He's worried about her, but he's not sure if it's because he actually feels concern for her or because he knows he's supposed to. She's fading, and he doesn't know what to do. He has no training, couldn't begin to guess how deep the knife is, or how close it is to her heart.

James has no self-control.

James either sent her down here to suffer with her pain and die, or he didn't care to be bothered with it any longer. Perhaps he didn't want to watch.

But it was Ellie's fault. Her anger was her downfall. And now that it's clear what they all were doing that night, Derek's not really all that surprised. It was obvious to him even back then that there was something to Whitney and Jackson. Now, he knows it was more than just feelings. It's silly how that one night made them run from each other. The two of them could've thrived from that shared experience. That's the kind of thing that makes you last. After all, that's what he was after, the kind of bond that can only be formed out of trauma.

Weakness. Everyone exposed theirs, forced to open themselves up to expose what they lack, everyone except for him. Even if he had come clean, control isn't a weakness, it's power. Ellie's is anger, of course. Jackson's is all in his head—

he lives too much in his mind, no follow through. Cowardice—that would be Whitney. Always letting someone else go first, always needing someone to hide behind, reliant on the direction of others. Without her safety nets, she would crumble. And James? It only took that one conversation in the office to figure out what makes him weak. His obsession. That fixation with the group, but mostly with Derek, or rather Derek's ability to produce a desired outcome. When there were so many other kids that came to this house and so many other kids who blew him off, what other reason would he have to fixate on them if not for Derek? Admittedly, he does have some will power, enough to stalk them for years, but now that his plan is in motion, he's falling apart.

A throaty gurgle escapes Ellie's mouth, and Derek gently lays her on the stone floor. There's nowhere else to put her. None that he can see in this darkness. He settles down on the ground beside her. She sat with him just hours ago when he was bloodied on the floor; now, he supposes it's his turn.

Memories of her float through his mind, rewinding all the way back to the beginning. Jackson will take it the worst; he's always been a brother figure for her. He smiles a little thinking of her in her prime when they were so much younger. The way her long hair would swish behind her as she ran to find a hiding spot during Hide-and-Seek or the way she could catch someone off guard with her large, sparkling eyes and booming personality. She was smart; he told her so many times that she just lacked focus. She never would have been failing if it weren't for that anger. It didn't always hit, but when it did, it consumed her. Grudges never had to build up for her to explode.

Ellie's fate is sealed. She's been banished to the cellar. James won't return to her now. But there are still two alive. Two who need to be saved and one who needs to be taught. Running his hands through her soft hair, Derek leans down to kiss her cheek. Swiftly, he jerks the knife from her chest, wipes it off on his pants, and calmly heads back up the stairs.

43

Blinking a few times, Jackson shakes his head, trying to clear it. He no longer has any sense of time. He can't see out the windows, and he doesn't wear a watch. All he knows is that he woke up here in this house of horrors, head pounding in agony. A trickle of sweat runs down his forehead and into his eye, and when it drops onto his shirt, he realizes it's blood, not sweat. Swiping it off his forehead is a relief. James forgot to retie their ropes, or maybe he didn't feel the need. At this point, Jackson's so banged up and dizzy; what can he possibly do to free them?

"Whit," he whispers. Collapsed and curled in on herself on the floor, she doesn't rouse. "Whit!" He tries again. His head is throbbing so much, he may vomit if he tries to stand, so he maneuvers the clunky boot under him and half slides, half crawls to where she lay. Positioning himself in front of her, he sits guard, her protector. At the very least, he can die trying to save her.

The smell in the room is impossible to ignore, and he looks down, noticing the stains on his shirt, and realizes the stench is coming from him. Hungry Man dinner and blood. His mind reels, bringing him back to dinner, back to James's ranting. Back to Ellie. The knife. He breaks; an anguished sob rips from his core, and once the tears start, they're impossible to stop. He doesn't know if Ellie is alive or dead, and he can't bear it. It's a nightmare; they're living in a nightmare. What will he say to her parents, his second family? Will their daughter come home? He was just beginning to repair a friendship that should never have been lost. Desperately, he forces himself to reign it in; Whitney is here and alive, unconscious but alive, and Melody needs her mother. His only job now is to make sure Whitney makes it out.

Hunched in pain, he sits guard in front of Whitney. As time moves on, the tears cleanse the ache from his head but not from his body and heart. The floor is dirty and hard; he tries to change his position until the discomfort becomes unbearable. He has to pee. He almost laughs at the absurdity of it, how strange it is to have such a normal need when you're trapped in a house with a psychopath. His lips mash together into a thin line and he wonders what to do. He doesn't want to leave her alone, but he has to go. He refuses to piss himself. That would only serve as entertainment to James. The small lamp doesn't illuminate much; it's hard to see, but it looks like a shadow on the wall across from the bed. A closet, or bathroom, maybe? Carefully, he moves his boot under his leg, putting as much weight on it as he can take, until he gets up to a mostly standing position. He's taken a beating, and the boot is most certainly slowing him down, but to take it off would be too painful to move. He hobbles and slides his way toward the shadow. Relief floods him when he sees it is in fact a door. His hand rests on the frame as he hefts his body inside. It's pitch dark, but with his other hand out, he connects with a sink. Thankful for small miracles, he feels his way into the room until he bumps into the toilet. He shivers, not wanting to imagine what the room looks like under working lights. Making it to the bathroom gives him dignity; it's defiant. As he's finishing up, he hears a creak from the bedroom. It grows louder, the door.

Scrambling to get himself together and make his way back to the bathroom door, he shoves the pain down deep. He's got to get back to Whitney. He can't lose her. He comes out of the bathroom to see James standing over her. James turns and smiles; the dim light from the lamp seems to stretch the sadistic smile across his face, and he looks like the devil himself. His eyes sparkle with excitement. A man whose last thread has just been cut. Whatever restraint he had disappeared when that knife sunk into Ellie's chest. He eagerly winds a long link of thick chains around his hands, his sights set on Whitney's unconscious form.

The world turns on its side as Jackson screams, running and tripping straight for James. Brown flecks of wallpaper and dust rain down on them as he crashes into James and manages to turn himself so that they land in a pile on the floor next to Whitney instead of on top of her. The chains clink and dance, almost making music as the two scuffle. Laughter rises from deep inside of James, and Jackson knows that if he ever makes it out of here, that will be the sound that will haunt him forever. His back hits the floor with a horrifying crunch as James flips him over, leering down at him. Tiny spit bubbles gather in the corners of James's mouth, and the chains dangle from his fingertips, swinging and taunting Jackson.

I'm not going to die like this.

He wonders what will happen to Whitney if James kills him? Injured and bloody, he fights with everything he has. As he throws fists and elbows, his mind repeats one sentence over and over.

He won't win.

Landing a solid punch, he's able to throw James a little to the left, freeing his leg. With a yell, he pulls his leg to his chest and throws his boot straight out into James's face, sending him flying across the room. Jackson scrambles up. Racing toward him, he grabs the chains from James's hands, but James is undeterred. Jackson twists the chains, trying to wind them around James's neck. He can't get it tight enough; James fights back. They shove, throwing themselves at each other. But then suddenly, James isn't fighting back any longer. his emotionless eyes stare straight at Jackson. Drool drips from his mouth as he slumps forward, and Jackson pulls the chains tighter and tighter and tighter.

"Jackson! Jackson, stop!" Derek's face swims into his vision. His fingers tremble as he forces them open to release the chains. He looks down at James, slumped forward, angry red slashes across his neck, and his own knife sticking out from between his shoulder blades. A fresh wave of the nauseating metallic smell of blood hits him all over again. He doubles over, dry-heaving.

"Jackson!" Derek races over, shaking him by the shoulders. "We have to get out of here; let's go!"

"Whitney," Jackson whispers. "Can you carry her?"

Derek turns to find Whitney still lying on the floor. "Is she?"

"Knocked out, but she's alive. We need to call an ambulance."

With the tip of his shoe, Derek nudges James's body, turning him to the side. He bends down, thrusting his hands into James's pants pockets.

"What are you doing?" Jackson shouts.

"The keys." Holding up a pair of tiny silver keys, Derek smiles with relief. "To get our phones." He pockets them and rushes to Whitney's side. "Alright, let's get her outside." Gently, he lifts her off the floor, throwing her body over his shoulder, carrying her out of the dark room, down the hall, and out the front door, and away from the house for the last time. Jackson limps behind him.

It's grown dark out, the moon is swallowed up in the clouds. A natural darkness, freeing, nothing like the orchestrated dark from inside, that made time disappear. The wind blows through his hair as Derek lays Whitney down on the cold, brittle grass.

"Stay here," he says to Jackson. "I'm going back to get our phones."

"Wait! What about Ellie? Is she okay?"

Even in the dark, Derek can see the watery eyes full of hope while Jackson waits for his answer.

"No," he shakes his head and turns, racing back into the house.

44

Thankful for James's collection of battery-powered lamps, Derek is able to pick his way back to the office and unlock the cabinet. He wonders about the notifications on their phones. Will anyone realize they've been missing? Probably not, their families all knew they had plans tonight. The only one not returning home will be Ellie. Something he will have to figure out how to handle later. He didn't want to lose her, but he couldn't save her.

Something nags at him; he should feel triumphant. He won. He beat James. Whitney and Jackson will forever think of him as their hero, but it's not just James. It's the house, and he can't let it win. It took Ellie, it took years from his own life, his friendships. Haunted or not, it doesn't get to win because it's not so much the house that was ever haunted, it was the feeling it gave. The person it produced. The house is the reason for all of this.

He shoves the phones in his pockets and calmly returns to the dining room, surveying the vile scene spread out before him. A mystery dinner theater set. All horror and no mystery. Without another thought, he grabs a candle from where James's plate still lies and holds it to a rope left dangling from a chair. He holds it steady until the rope catches. Lifting the candle to his face, he stares into the flame, savoring its warmth and power, before dropping it. He lets it fall to the floor, amongst the dirt, dust, glass, and whatever else has been left by all of the many other kids who have trampled through here, having left it no better, no worse than they did.

The fire spreads quickly; he races outside to see Whitney waking up, a piece of wallpaper falls from her hair as Jackson leans in to kiss her cheek. It's exactly as he imagined nine years ago; their arms outstretched, they grab ahold of him, huddling together close as they fumble with their phones to call for help. Another room goes up in flames, and they watch through tears and hugs, and when the office begins to burn, Derek smiles. It may have taken nine years to get here, but he got it done.

After all, you don't just get a happy ending; you have to earn it.

Other titles by BLKDOG Publishing for your consideration:

Wendell
By Amy-Brooke Odell

Wendell is just a kid trying to enjoy his life in the mountains of North Carolina. Things are hard because his mother; Vera, left when he was only a baby. She was known throughout town to be a little bit odd, obsessed with folklore and town mythology, and the school bullies don't like to let him forget it. As hard as the bullies can be on him, Wendell has two best friends and a loving grandmother that have filled his life, until now.

When Wendell begins to show curiosity in the town's legend of the Wind Folk, Granny Dess tries to dissuade him to keep him from ending up like his mother. Granny Dess feels he would be happier if he would look toward the future and not the past. She does whatever she can to try to make sure that he doesn't get caught up in what she considers foolishness and fantasy. But, after witnessing some very strange and magical occurrences, Wendell's curiosity wins out and he begins to secretly search for information into the town's infamous legend.

Wendell and his friends, both human and animal, embark on a journey to discover the truth about the Wind Folk and where his mother really is. His world of baseball, camp-outs, and fishing is rocked when he discovers that the adults in town know a lot more than they say, and sometimes those tales told around a campfire are true. And, when it comes to the Wind Folk; it is said if you see one, you become one.

Maxwell's History of the World in 366 Lessons
By M. J. Trow

Peter Maxwell is the History teacher you wish you'd had. If you meet anyone (and you will) who says 'I hate History. It's boring,' they weren't taught by Mad Max.

Many of you will know him as the crime-solving sleuth (along with his police-person wife, Jacquie) in the Maxwell series by M.J. Trow (along with *his* non-policeperson wife, Carol, aka Maryanne Coleman – uncredited!) but what he is *paid* to do is teach History. And to that end has brought – and continues to bring – culture to thousands.

In his 'blog' (Dinosaur Maxwell doesn't really know what that is) written in 2012, the year in which the world was supposed to end, but mysteriously didn't, you will find all sorts of fascinating factoids about the *only* important subject on the school curriculum. So, if you weren't lucky enough to be taught by Max, or you've forgotten all the History you ever knew, here is your chance to play catch-up. The 'blog' has been edited by Maxwell's friend, the crime writer M.J. Trow, who writes almost as though he knows what the Great Man was thinking.

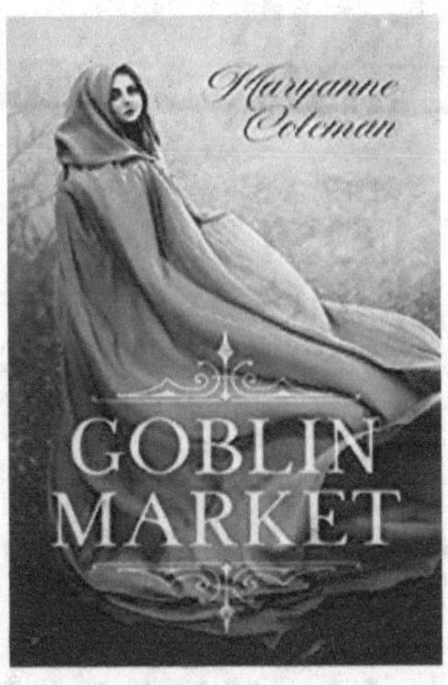

Goblin Market
By Maryanne Coleman

Have you ever wondered what happened to the faeries you used to believe in? They lived at the bottom of the garden and left rings in the grass and sparkling glamour in the air to remind you where they were. But that was then – now you might find them in places you might not think to look. They might be stacking shelves, delivering milk or weighing babies at the clinic. Open your eyes and keep your wits about you and you might see them.

But no one is looking any more and that is hard for a Faerie Queen to bear and Titania has had enough. When Titania stamps her foot, everyone in Faerieland jumps; publicity is what they need. Television, magazines. But that sort of thing is much more the remit of the bad boys of the Unseelie Court, the ones who weave a new kind of magic; the World Wide Web. Here is Puck re-learning how to fly; Leanne the agent who really is a vampire; Oberon's Boys playing cards behind the wainscoting; Black Annis, the bag-lady from Hainault, all gathered in a Restoration comedy that is strictly twenty-first century.

Prester John: Africa's Lost King
By Richard Denham

He sits on his jewelled throne on the Horn of Africa in the maps of the sixteenth century. He can see his whole empire reflected in a mirror outside his palace. He carries three crosses into battle and each cross is guarded by one hundred thousand men. He was with St Thomas in the third century when he set up a Christian church in India. He came like a thunderbolt out of the far East eight centuries later, to rescue the crusaders clinging on to Jerusalem. And he was still there when Portuguese explorers went looking for him in the fifteenth century.

Was he real? Did he ever exist? This book will take you on a journey of a lifetime, to worlds that might have been, but never were. It will take you, if you are brave enough, into the world of Prester John.

Fade
By Bethan White

There is nothing extraordinary about Chris Rowan. Each day he wakes to the same faces, has the same breakfast, the same commute, the same sort of homes he tries to rent out to unsuspecting tenants.

There is nothing extraordinary about Chris Rowan. That is apart from the black dog that haunts his nightmares and an unexpected encounter with a long forgotten demon from his past. A nudge that will send Chris on his own downward spiral, from which there may be no escape.

There is nothing extraordinary about Chris Rowan...

The Children's Crusade
By M. J. Trow

In the summer of 1212, 30,000 children from towns and villages all over France and Germany left their homes and families and began a crusade. Their aim; to retake Jerusalem, the holiest city in the world, for God and for Christ. They carried crosses and they believed, because the Bible told them so, that they could cross the sea like Moses. The walls of Jerusalem would fall, like Jericho's did for Joshua.

It was the age of miracles – anything was possible. Kings ignored the Children; so did popes and bishops. The handful of Church chroniclers who wrote about them were usually disparaging. They were delusional, they were inspired not by God, but the Devil. Their crusade was doomed from the start.

None of them reached Outremer, the Holy Land. They turned back, exhausted. Some fell ill on the way; others died. Others still were probably sold into slavery to the Saracens – the very Muslims who had taken Jerusalem in the first place.

We only know of three of them by name – Stephen, Nicholas and Otto. One of them was a shepherd, another a ploughboy, the third a scholar. The oldest was probably fourteen. Today, in a world where nobody believes in miracles, the Children of 1212 have almost been forgotten.

Almost… but not quite…

The poet Robert Browning caught the mood in his haunting poem, *The Pied Piper of Hamelin*, bringing to later readers the sad image of a lost generation, wandering a road to who knew where.

Weirdest War Two
By Richard Denham & M. J. Trow

Was Britain's Thermopylae really fought over a tennis court?

What happened in Canada during the invasion of Winnipeg?

How did the Night Witches terrify and torment the Axis?

Was Hitler actually sent to spy on the Nazis by the army?

Who was the schoolgirl who helped win the Battle of Britain?

Truth, they say, is the first casualty of war. You will have to decide how many such casualties occur in this book, the third in the *Weird War* series. Amber rooms worth a fortune, the spear that pierced Christ's side, deadly female snipers and Lucille Ball's spooky teeth, it's all here for the discerning buff of 1939-45.

Whether it's official Nazi propaganda dreamed up by Josef Goebbel's Ministry of Enlightenment or the 'scuttlebutt' of the US navy; tall stories from the officers' mess or attempts to escape from the grim reality of total war, the Second World War

provides a fascinating glimpse into the mindset and ingenuity of
a generation.

Have we now exhausted our supply of weirdness? With new
information coming to light all the time from the classified
archives in the corridors of power, we wouldn't bet on it!

www.blkdogpublishing.com